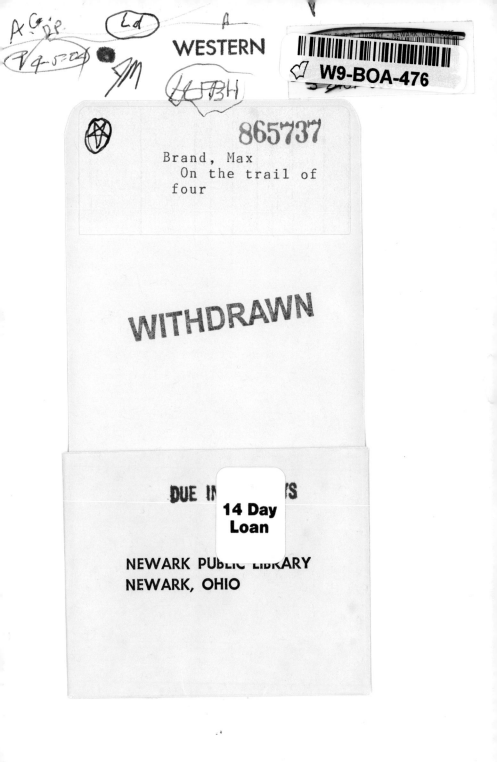

WESTERN

W9-BOA-476

865737

Brand, Max
   On the trail of
four

WITHDRAWN

DUE IN ~~~~~S

14 Day
Loan

NEWARK PUBLIC LIBRARY
NEWARK, OHIO

ON THE TRAIL
OF FOUR

Max Brand

THORNDIKE PRESS • THORNDIKE, MAINE

Library of Congress Cataloging in Publication Data:

Brand, Max, 1892–1944
  On the trail of four

  1. Large type books. I. Title.
[PS3511.A87O5   1985]   813'.52   84–26885
ISBN 0–89621–607–1 (lg. print)

Copyright 1925 by Street and Smith Corporation, under the
name of David Manning.
Copyright renewed, 1953, by Dorothy Faust.
All rights reserved.
No part of this book may be reproduced in any form
without permission in writing from the publisher.

Large Print edition available through arrangement with
Dodd, Mead, & Company, New York.

Cover design by Mimi Harrison

ON THE TRAIL
OF FOUR

865737

882787

CHAPTER 1

I had seen the cabin before, two or three times. It had been thrown up, within the last six months, by an old sour-dough prospector who had located a rift of pay dirt on the face of a mountain of quartzite. There he had been pegging away ever since. I suppose that his coffee mill ground out three or four dollars a day, but that was enough for him. Every two months or so he went down from the mountainside, herding his burro before him. He came into the town and there he always managed to discover whisky and drank enough of it to reach a fairly mellowed condition – that is to say, he put away a quart or more of raw stuff.

After that, he bought what he needed to float him through the next two months – powder, caps, fuse, molasses, flour, and bacon. There were not many essentials in the life of such a man as "Truck" Janvers. But the taste of pone and molasses was like a sweet dream leading me on as I struggled ahead for the cabin.

I say that I was struggling, and I was. It did not make much difference that I had beneath me the surest-footed mule that ever cat-jumped up the face of a precipice, hanging on by the toes of his hoofs. Spike would have had to be a mind reader and prophet combined to make anything out of the trail which we were trying to follow.

The reason was that the upper mountains were blanketed in the dark of the night and in smoke-thick fog. All that I could do was to keep Spike near the big wall of the upper mountain and then simply trust to luck to bring me right at the end of the trail.

There is nothing so baffling as mountain fog – which is simply a cloud that floats no higher than the elevation at which one happens to be traveling. For the very reason that we of the mountains generally expect crystal-clear weather, a fog is an almost unnerving nuisance.

Now and again I got my head above the level of the sea of white. It was not a thick stratum of cloud, but what there was of it was as opaque as clouded quartz. When my head was above the smoke I could see the bright cold stars above me and the blue-black of the midnight sky.

Cold stars, and cold fog. How under heaven that fog could have been so cold without turning into snow and falling, I cannot understand. My nose and chin were almost frozen and the breath I drew into my lungs seemed to congeal and turn to ice there. My hands grew numb. I wrapped the reins around the pommel of the saddle – though I knew very well that that is a dangerous expedient – and I let Spike do pretty much as he pleased.

After all, that mule had about as much sense as most mountain-wise men. I had only one thing to guide me. I knew that the cabin lay in the neighborhood of a hundred yards above the edge of the trees. My plan was simply to zigzag back and forth, covering a hundred yards or more out, and then combing carefully back to the trees and starting once more.

That sounds like a simple proceeding, and under ordinary conditions it would have been. But with the feeling that I was freezing to death and that I had to make haste – and with the knowledge that unless I came actually blundering upon the cabin I should miss it altogether – and above all with a wild sense of confusion owing to the fog, I suppose that I must have traced and retraced my steps a dozen times in the next hour and a half. In fact, I had direct evidence that I had done so when I looked about me the next day.

I wondered, however, that I did not see some token of a light breaking through the blind wall of the fog, for on other occasions before this, as I had sent Spike swinging over the lower lands of the valley beneath, I had looked up even at midnight and seen the ray of light from the miner's cabin like a thin wand of yellow, pointed down to me. Probably Truck Janvers was one of those who stayed up late at night to read yarns in the magazines. However, though it was now not more than half-past eight, there was no sign of a light near me.

All sorts of illusions come into the mind of a man in a fog, just as they come into the mind of a man in a waiting room. I felt that that infernal cabin must have slid off the face of the mountain and smashed to bits in the ravine beneath. I almost hoped that it had, in my vexation.

But then, with a thud and a snort, Spike found the log wall. I swung myself down from the saddle with more groans than any rusted door.

"Hey, Janvers!" I called.

Then I paused. I had never spoken to this fellow. One never could tell. It was true that the reputation of Hugo Ames stood fairly high among the outlying dwellers of those high places, and I knew that Janvers could not help having heard of me – also that he could never have heard that I had ever injured or stuck-up any lonely shepherd, miner, or trapper. They were not my "meat." On the whole, therefore, I was reassured. But truly assured I could not be, any more than any man upon whose head the price of fifteen thousand dollars hangs, alive or dead.

Fifteen thousand dollars!

Well, I was not shivering with the cold long before I finished that train of thought. Yet, I decided that this night was too horribly wet and cold to attempt to make a camp in the dripping forest if I could possibly avoid it. I blundered on toward that shack and found that I had come to the rear of it. I had to feel my way around two corners before I reached the front – with Spike following obediently behind me.

Then I came to the door, and I found it closed. I rattled the latch and called: "Janvers! Hey, Truck!"

I got no answer to this hail. I yelled again at the top of my lungs, and when I received no response this time, I decided that Truck must have started down to the town that night and decided not to return through the fog. At any rate, that was no good reason why I should not go in and cook myself a few slices of bacon and a cup of coffee, to say nothing of a mouthful of cold pone which I might find in the bread box.

I opened the latch without any difficulty and stepped in. I shouted once more, because Truck, being on in years, might be a little deaf and a very heavy sleeper.

"Truck Janvers!"

I called at the top of my lungs, but I got nothing in response but the deep, sudden echo of my own voice roaring back at me and instantly stilled. Then I lighted a match. There was no Janvers there – he had left in a hurry, apparently, for yonder was a table tilted over against the wall, and here were two chairs overturned. I was about to take a step forward when an instinct in my very flesh made me look down. There lay Janvers at my feet, with crimson stains on his gray hair!

I had the two lanterns lighted instantly. In such a case one needs plenty of light before one attempts to see what has happened. Then I kneeled over him.

One bullet had struck him in the breast and come out under his shoulder blade behind. Another bullet had struck his body lower down. As I ripped away his shirt I discovered these things. The second bullet had not come out. But, by the position of both wounds, I guessed very safely that either of them would have been enough to soak the life out of poor Truck Janvers. The wounds were still bleeding. There was still a ray of life left in him, but it was already twinkling, and it would soon be out.

Yet if I could fan that to a momentary fire and learn the name of his murderer – that would be an end worth while. This was the sort of a case that would make Sheriff Jud Hawkins spend sleepless days and nights of labor until he had solved it. For it was his boast that a poor man was more promptly avenged than a rich one, in his county.

I thought of trying bandages. But I saw that that would be a useless formality. Probably the pain would kill him instantly. Besides, he was not bleeding fast. I had a flask of brandy which I carried with me constantly – Mexican brandy, colorless as water and terrible as nitroglycerin. I wedged open the hard-gripped teeth of the miner and poured a dam of that awful pale brandy down his throat. He gasped feebly. Then he managed to swallow the stuff. I tried him with a second swig, and his dazed eyes slowly opened wide and looked out blankly at me.

I heaved him up. He was a burden even to my arms. I sat him up in a chair against the wall. Still he watched me with sagging mouth and with those dreadful, dying eyes – as though he was struggling to make out my features at a great distance.

"Janvers!" I shouted at him. "Wake up and talk – who did it to you?"

There was a faint gleam in his eyes, I thought. But no words came. He made a numb movement with his lips, but only a gasp came from his throat.

I tried the brandy again – I put half the flask down his throat, and with that half pint of liquid fire in him, he began to show a sign of life. His eyelids fluttered over his dull eyes, and a groan left his lips.

In the white, blind night outside, Spike echoed that groan with a snort, as though he had stumbled against a rock.

"Who did it, Janvers?" I shouted to him.

His head wobbled over to one side. Life was dropping out of him fast, but he began to speak with a great effort.

"My boy – San Marin –"

Then a whisper passed under the pit of my arm as I leaned over him and a heavy knife buried itself in the hollow of the throat of Janvers. He dropped back in the chair, dead! He rolled heavily from the chair and fell on the floor upon his face.

I was on the floor myself, by that time, which

is the safest place by all odds in time of such emergency, but I was facing the door with my revolver stretched out before me. There was nothing but the solid sheet of the fog and one long arm of white mist, reaching into the cabin as though that was the ghostly arm which had just flung the knife into the throat of the miner.

Then, blindly, I ran out into the night, but three steps through blanketing mist assured me that I was playing the part of a fool. Whoever had flung that knife or fired the shots into the body of Janvers, I could not locate them in such weather as this. I turned back slowly to the cabin and went in again.

CHAPTER 2

If I could not immediately follow after the murderers, I could at least make sure what had been the motive of this cold-blooded crime, to complete which the assassin had sneaked back and thrown the knife. Perhaps, through a thinning of the fog, as he hurried away he saw the glimmer of the light from the cabin and knew that some one was there – some one who might take advantage of a dying whisper of the other. So the final touch had been given.

I cannot tell you how infuriating it was to me. It was not the first time, of course, that I had seen death. Though I was not half so familiar with it as those fools who wrote articles for newspapers and magazines about "red-handed Hugo Ames, the outlaw." But I had never witnessed a death that took me so by the throat – that had so much ghostly terror about it. A great deal of pathos, too, for I couldn't imagine this dead man as a villain in the life of any one.

I went mechanically through the shack. There was not the least doubt, of course, that the crime had been committed not for revenge, but on account of the poor little pittance of gold old Truck Janvers had been able to grind out with his coffee mill in the past month or so.

Yet I went through the cabin, turning things over with an idle hand, because there was nothing else for me to do, in the white blanket of the fog that lay over the world outside. Finally, miserably concealed in a corner of the hut, I stumbled onto a little box, and in the box a canvas bag, and in the bag a small handful of sparkling yellow dust – here was the treasure of poor Janvers.

Here was the only motive for which I could imagine a murder. I sifted the stuff carelessly back and forth in my hands, and some of it spilled onto my clothes. I cared nothing about the stuff itself. But if there was no money motive behind the killing, what was the reason?

It was not a very cheerful situation in which to consider a murder mystery. The drifting forms in the white mist beyond the open door sent shudders of apprehension through me. I restored the gold to its former place with a shudder.

Another possibility leaped into my mind. It was possible that the vein which Janvers was working had opened out into a rich streak and that some one, envying his fortune, had decided to steal from him the source of the gold rather than the gold itself. But this was a thing which I could not investigate further until the daylight came and I could enter his hole in the ground.

Yet it seemed most highly improbable that old Truck, with his fondness for hard liquor, would be wasting golden moments on the side of the hill when here in the sack was enough to take him to the village to celebrate his discovery!

I turned from the cabin to Truck himself. His blunt face and high, Scandinavian cheekbones were certainly not easily to be associated with mystery of any kind.

So I went through his pockets. I found odds and ends – nothing else. In his wallet there were three much-soiled and crumpled dollar bills. There were a couple of clippings from newspapers – foolish cartoons which had caught the eye of the simple fellow. There was a letter, as well. The envelope had rubbed to tatters and a mass of pulp. The outer fold of the letter itself was a blurred mass of ink which no eyes in the world could have deciphered as writing.

I opened it without interest, but, the moment it was unfolded, I was truly startled to find within a man's handwriting, but a handwriting of the finest quality – well formed and flowing – a handwriting young, rich in character – the sort of writing which one might associate with a man of talent – talent in some handicraft. The writing of a gentleman, I thought it was, as well.

All of this was the more intriguing, of course, because as far as I had heard of Janvers – and he had been in these mountains for ten years at least – he hardly knew a handful of people who could pass as civilized.

Then again, there was a renewed interest because this was a familiar letter.

. . . but afterward, I grew tired of such
a way of life, Truck . . .

Those were the first words that I could make out. I turned to the signature and found: "Crinky."

That was another poser. The sort of nickname one could give to a girl, say – a little girl. What the devil had a man by the name of Crinky to do with this rough-handed old miner and prospector?

I scratched my head over that and then I

went back to the reading of the letter itself. But who had ever heard of such a name as Crinky? No one that I know! There was something rather catchy about the name – a token of affection, you might almost say. At least, that was how I read it in that cabin, beside the dead man. You will see that my mind was reaching after very small clues indeed!

I began with the letter where I had left off:

. . . I grew tired of such a way of life, Truck, I had to settle down in some way. You know the rest.

I know that you don't approve of what I have decided on. I know why you don't approve. But I ask you to remember two things. The first is that I'm not the same fellow you used to know. I think that you would be almost proud to recognize me, now. The second is that people down here in San Marin haven't the same outlook on life that you have. They aren't so stern. They don't expect so much of a man – especially of a young man.

If I haven't been a model – well, I'll admit all of that. I haven't been industrious, either. I've been as full of faults as a haystack is full of straws. But then, you know that a man can change. Look at your own life!

I suppose that I should not leave that in the letter for fear that it might anger you, but I presume, after all, that you are too fair and square to mind frank talk. At least, you have always been very frank with me.

Perhaps, at the base, you are entirely right. But remember that every man will try to live. There's that instinct in us. I am merely fighting to live.

You must not smile at that. When I say that I am fighting to live, I mean just that. Other people may be able to scratch out an existence and call it life. But I cannot be satisfied with that. I must live beautifully or else I do not care to live at all.

You can destroy my chance of happiness. You can destroy my chance of becoming a good and a useful man! It needs only a word from you to do it. But for the sake of mercy, let me go on in my own way. At the worst, I shall never draw you into my affairs again. As ever,

Crinky

What a letter and what a signature!

I sat there and brooded over that missive for a long time. I should have been certain that this was a letter which Janvers had picked up and with which he had nothing to do. But he was

21

named in the very first line of it!

An easy letter, a humble letter, a gentle letter, and yet a desperate letter, too. I guessed that there might be steel claws behind this velvet if Crinky were cornered.

And that name, Crinky! A devilish odd and intriguing name. But what had it to do with that dead bull, Truck Janvers?

Finally I put the letter carefully back into his pocket. I did not need it any more. I knew every word of it by heart and I also knew that I should repeat that letter a hundred times, unconsciously, until it was printed in my flesh, so to speak.

However that may be, I knew suddenly and perfectly why Truck Janvers had been killed. He was able to stretch out his hand from the distance and forbid that happiness toward which Crinky was aspiring.

What did that happiness of Crinky consist in? Some guilty thing, no doubt. Perhaps the power of Truck over this stranger was his knowledge of the stranger's past.

However, I had not failed to note in the letter of Crinky a certain gentle and appealing tone. It was hard for me, even out of written words, to imagine this as a man capable of serious crimes.

But on the spot I made up my mind that I

could not rest, until I had followed the name of Crinky around the entire world and located the owner of it at last. I had one clue which might work out in the beginning.

"My boy – San Marin –"

In the town of San Marin, therefore, I intended to hunt for news first of all. But where was San Marin? How could I, an outlawed man, travel safely toward it, and into a country where I knew nothing of the people or the landscape? Madness, you will say, for me to slip out of my hole-in-the-wall country where I was familiar with every crevice, and risk myself abroad.

Well, I thought of all these things, but in the end I knew that I could not resist the temptation. I had to ride on that trail, no matter where it took me.

It was not that I had any particular fondness for Truck. Of course he was almost an utter stranger to me; but the crime against him was what fascinated me. I guessed at a vast power of evil behind the crime. But oh, if I could have had a hint of the real blackness behind the knife which struck him down, I should never have been able to wrap myself in my blankets that night and sleep in the cabin on the floor beside the murdered man.

CHAPTER 3

It was not strange that I wakened after a short sleep, an hour before sunrise. The fog had cleared. First I took Truck's burro. It was hobbled, which was fair proof that it had a hankering to move toward some other place than "home." Perhaps it was bought from some one in the village in the valley below. At any rate, I had to take a chance. If I hoped to get on the trail of the murderer, I could not wait to bury the body of Janvers. I merely saddled the burro and pinned a great piece of paper on the side of the saddle:

TRUCK JANVERS LIES MURDERED IN HIS CABIN

Then I turned the burro loose and clipped it along the side. It made an honest effort to plant its hard little hoofs in the middle of my brow, but my boxing training helped me to side-step, and the heels darted over my shoulder. Then I was glad to see the little beast jog down the trail toward the village. That contrary-minded burro would not hurry even toward liberty!

After that was done, I cut for the sign of the murderer. I found my own sign – oceans of it. I had tied up my trail in a delightfully foolish tangle the night before, as I could see. But I had to work for a long time, and the morning light was bright before I found what I wanted. At a considerable distance from the shack, and over the brow of the ridge, I found a great pool of horse tracks. And from this pool a trail led away, covered by the prints of no fewer than four horses.

It was very interesting! For one thing, it gave me no fear that the trail would be any too difficult to follow, or that the speed of that retiring party would be any too great. I don't think that I ever saw a body of four horsemen who could escape from me if I had even an ordinary horse for the pursuit. Four always ride slower than the slowest horse in the party. For there is only one reason for getting ahead in every mind in a party, but there are four reasons for lingering at whatever comes in the trail. There are four heads to be consulted in the solution of every problem.

Well, being contented with what I had seen, I went back and cooked a breakfast. You will think that it was a rather gruesome thing to sit quietly by and cook a meal while a dead man lay stretched in the cabin beside me. But I hardly saw him. I only saw the mystery before me, and all the deepening wonders which were attached to it. For, you see, the fact that four riders had come to strike down poor Truck Janvers, was enough to raise the killing above a normal murder.

They had ridden up through the night, deliberately. In the first place, they had reconnoitered the situation with the greatest care. They were so sure of themselves and the direction in which they were traveling, that a fog which had baffled me and a good mount that I was on did not bother them at all. They had proceeded through the mist as straight as though they were following a guiding light. In spite of the sheltering fog – or for fear lest it might suddenly thin or lift in a puff of wind – they had halted their horses beyond the ridge. Then they had stolen ahead to the cabin – one or more.

I could not find any traces of their feet. To be sure, the soil around the cabin was extremely rocky, but even so, their ability to move up to the cabin in the night without leaving a single sign rather bewildered me. Although, for that matter, I have never been an Indian when it comes to trailing. Some people are endowed with an extra sense in that matter; but no white man has ever attained the perfection of good Indians.

At any rate, I decided that the trail proved one thing at least: Which was that these people had ridden straight toward Truck Janvers with the agreed purpose of destroying the miner. There was nothing haphazard about the matter. They had not ridden past the cabin, but only up to it, and then they had doubled straight back. Truck Janvers had been a dead man, in their minds, a long time before the two bullets and the knife ended him.

Furthermore, I felt that the four had acted with such caution, that I had to deal with impulsive brutality under the influence of whisky, but with a very cold, steady murderousness which it was hard to conceive. How could such a simple fellow as Janvers have offended four men enough to make them ride by night to do away with him without a fighting chance?

You will see why it was that I forgot the body of Truck himself. I ate my breakfast in a brown study, and then I saddled and mounted Spike and started. It was easy trailing, for a time. Then the trail hit a stretch of rocks and there were difficulties. I hit straight across the rocks to the soft dirt on the farther side, but I cut for sign in vain there. I had to work far to the left before I found what I wanted.

This was more interesting still. The four were determined to make their trail as difficult as possible. Even as early as this, they were making little problems which would break the heart of any hasty pursuit.

I labored down that trail all day, and I assure you that my hands were full. Every instant I had to be using my wits. Sometimes the four sets of signs were unwoven − first one strand going apart and then another, and then another, until the straight course of the riders was marked out by one horseman only. This fellow would lead me into a nest of rocks, or into a stream, create a trail problem that made my head ache for an hour, and then away would go his sign at a sharp angle, to rejoin the others who, meeting again, had gone off at high speed!

Indeed, they galloped so much that I began to suspect these fellows must be Mexicans, for few Americans, even cowpunchers, push horses as hard as Mexicans do.

All that day I worked, and far into the dusk. Then I camped, exhausted. It was a dry camp and a miserable one on bleak highlands, combed by a biting wind. I was glad to be up again, shivering and cramped with cold. Off went Spike and I, as soon I could make out the sign again, and on into the morning we struggled.

A good deal of my enthusiasm for this work had left me, I confess, even so early in the game. For, in spite of my assurance as to riding faster with a poor mount than four men can ride with good ones, I had never had in mind four riders who were so skillful in concealing their tracks. I saw that the signs were much less fresh the farther I went. Every moment they were gaining! And trails dim quickly to the eyes of white men.

The morning grew hotter and hotter, and my discontent grew greater and greater. But I kept to the faint trail. They had obviously turned onto the road here, and followed it as it wound down into the green heart of the valley beneath. Yes, and perhaps they had followed it where it wound across the valley and struggled up the farther mountainside.

At any rate, it was worth the trial, and I decided that I would make the short cut. My heart was in my mouth when I rode Spike slowly toward the edge of the cliff and looked down to the mountainside, all jagged and toothed with rocks and boulders. But Spike had no such doubts. He strained against the bit until he had stretched out his long neck. Then down he pitched for the bottom of the valley, caroming from one precarious footing to another.

I waved my hand and shouted like a madman. Indeed, it was as though I were sitting on the back of an eagle for that wild descent. Suddenly, we were sloping smoothly out on the floor of the valley beneath.

I had been right in this guess, at least. Where the road wound up the side of the opposite mountain I found their trail as big as life. I felt victory in my grip. Even by this one maneuver I must have gained a full half hour upon them, and if the trail were only long enough I knew that I should be able to overtake them. For no animal that ever carried man could live with my cat-footed mule when it came to a long-distance race over the highlands. I tried him on the mountain grade. Away he drove at that famous, long-swinging trot of his, and plowed steadily up to the top of the grade.

He was breathing a little; but it would have killed most horses to carry a two-hundred-pound man through such difficulties. I leaned and slapped the shoulder of Spike, and he tossed his head and pretended with flattened ears to be furious with me.

Then we struck away across the level on the trail. By the middle of the next day I promised myself that I should be on the heels of the four riders; and then let them protect themselves. For the murdered body of poor Truck Janvers lay heavily upon my mind's eye.

But I did not come up with them upon the middle of the next day. Neither did I come up with them upon the day following, or even on the day that still succeeded that. As I watched Spike swinging forward, I wondered what sort of winged creatures these could be that were flying before me and keeping him at a distance!

It was not until the fourth day thereafter that I had my first glimpse of them. But, when I saw them, I very well understood!

CHAPTER 4

I had risen early in the morning and, as the dawn light began in the east, I had dipped down into the heart of a narrow ravine. Then, rising against the horizon, black against that lovely flare of color, I saw four riders on four horses at the rim of the ground above me. They were the men after whom I was questing, and, the moment that I saw these horsemen, I understood very well why I had not been able to overtake the riders before.

It was at quite close range that I saw the riders, with such a light behind them that, though I could not make out features, yet the silhouette was wonderfully clear. I saw that those four horses were of a kingly breed, made like thoroughbreds, only that they were a little less leggy. I thought that they answered very nearly to my mind's picture of what an Arab must be like. At any rate, they were four beauties, and I gaped at them in bewilderment.

Mind you, I had only a flash of those horses before they drifted on out of sight, but that flash was all that I needed. If there was an animal there that was worth less than five hundred dollars, I was willing to call myself blind and a fool. Quality and breeding emanated from them like a light.

What were they doing, then, under such riders as these? Or were the four outlaws, perhaps? Yes, but if they were outlaws, was it possible that the four of them would undertake the peril and the fatigue of a march which I already knew had consumed a fortnight going and coming? Would the four of them have ridden this great distance all for the sake of putting to death one clumsy-handed miner who, it seemed to me, could have been safely handled by any cool-eyed boy?

No matter how I looked at the death of Janvers, it grew more and more maddening. I could not understand! I put my impatience behind me. Behind that problem lay some great meaning. Four such horses could not be owned by four common men. If these four men had ridden a thousand miles to kill a common old prospector, it was because his death meant a great deal indeed either to them or to some one who had hired them. It was all very well to tell myself this, but still I followed them with a hungry heart.

From that moment I had them repeatedly in sight. I found that I had to go with caution all the time, for I never knew when I might come into their view; for, once I had caught up with them, I found that they were really no match for Spike. Across the flat, to be sure, they simply walked away from him with matchless ease. But when it came to the sides of ravines, and the rough and tumble of cut up country, or when it came to plodding through deep, soft sand, then the matchless strength and the mule patience of Spike was too much for them. I was constantly drifting within sight of them during that day, but when the night came, I satisfied myself that I had not been seen by them.

After dark, however, I took the precaution of camping on a selected site. For that matter, after four years of a hunted life, it was instinct for me to protect myself as much as possible. I built no fire – not so much as a flame the size of the palm of my hand. I had a canteen of water and a slab of hardtack for my supper. Spike I put at a little distance from me among the brush, where he would be sure to find grass enough among the shrubbery. I knew, from of old, that he would not wander beyond the reach of my call. My own blanket I unrolled in the shelter of a nest of rocks and there I furled myself in it and folded my hands under my head with a good-night cigarette between my lips.

I was thinking of those four horses against the morning color – four marvelous pictures of beauty – and into the stillness of my thoughts came a rustling softer than the stir of a snake's belly across the ground.

Instantly, I was wide awake, and my legs were gathered under me. Then I waited, not drawing a breath. The sliding sound was gone, but I heard an instant later a very soft noise which I should not have perceived had I not tuned my ears to an extra sharpness – the light crunching made by a heavy body as foot or knee presses against the ground.

That was enough. I acted on the first impulse which came to me. A very foolish impulse, you will think, but I have found that in a crisis very often the boldest and the apparently wildest move is really the most safe. Above all, the hunter is never more confused than when he finds that he has changed roles and become the hunted!

I leaped into the air with a gun in either hand and with a wild yell breaking from my throat.

It gained me what I wanted – the sight of

two dim shadows crawling toward me among the rocks – and two quick exclamations of terror. But they were not so baffled that they could not act.

A gun blazed at me as I shot into the air like a jumping jack and a very honestly intentioned slug combed past my ear. I dodged as I landed, and fired from both hands. Whatever happened to one bullet, the other went home. It brought one of the creepers pitching to his feet with a scream, his arms flung into the air, and then he toppled backward.

I did not have to ask questions about him. That man was dead. The second, however, rising to his knees with a snarl, attempted to fire, and I heard the hammer click heavily, lifelessly. His gun had clogged. He did not pause. I saw the dull glimmer of steel as he tossed his gun aside and then he came at me with his hands.

I could have filled him with lead before he reached me, but there is something in me which has never let me shoot at a man without a gun in his hand. I dropped the Colt from my right hand and poised myself for the blow.

Aye, but this scoundrel did not intend an honest fight, hand to hand. At the last instant I saw the wicked gleam of the knife with which he was lunging at me. The thrill of that fear made me agile enough, I think. I dropped far down under the line of that stabbing knife and gave my man the benefit of two hundred and twenty pounds of reasonably hard muscle and bone all concentrated behind a flying right hand.

The blow caught him well down on the ribs, and I felt them crunch under the impact like an eggshell – a frightful feeling under my hand. There was weight enough in that punch to stop his mid-rush and flattened him on the ground and there he lay tied in a knot, kicking and gasping to regain his breath.

He would be perfectly helpless for some minutes. So I stepped to the first unlucky fellow and lighted a match to make sure of him. The flare of the light showed me a great tall fellow with a long, thin face, high features, and a sallow skin.

There was no use in examining his wound. I saw that the bullet had struck behind his neck, as he lay on the ground, and it must have ranged down into his vitals. It was only wonderful that it had left the instant of life in him which enabled him to leap to his feet and give his death cry.

I turned from him to a flurry in the brush. There I saw, suddenly, the figures of five animals rushing through the night, controlled by two riders.

Five – and one of them must be Spike.

I raised a mighty shout for him, and instantly one of the shadowy beasts detached itself from the rest and raced, riderless, toward me. The two riders followed Spike with a snap shot or two, but who can fire accurately from the back of a galloping horse?

At least, the scoundrels were away without doing me an injury, and having made up their minds that their two friends were lost, they were not remaining near to inquire after their hurts. The two were abandoned to my hands, to finish them in any way that I chose.

I came back to my second man – and just in time; for I found that, in spite of his half-winded lungs, and in spite of the agony which must be burning in his side, he had wormed himself over to a fallen revolver – my own – and he was gathering it into his hand when I kicked it out of his grip.

He turned on me with a snarl of such brute rage that I thrust him away with an exclamation of horror. Then I lighted the second match and saw the lean face of a Negro, as black as night!

I gave him not a bit more attention for the moment. There was no weapon near him, now. So I kindled a small fire as soon as I could bring together some dead brush. After the flame had warmed and grown to a comfortable point so that I could look over my captive, I sat down to watch him.

He lay flat on the ground, except for his shoulders, which were supported against a shelving edge of rock. The pain from his side, though it had not made him utter a cry, was nevertheless great enough to turn him to muddy gray. And yet I thought that there was more curiosity than malice in his glance as he stared back at me.

"So," said I, "we are all here together like good friends at the end of a hard day's work. What is your name, Tony?"

His eyes remained perfectly blank. I tried him in Spanish.

"What are you, friend?"

He nodded.

"Do you say friend?" said he, and he grinned a twisted smile.

"I say friend," said I. "Matter of habit. I'm an amiable sort of a fellow."

He tried to make a gesture of amused comment, but a pang in his side made him drop one hand to the hurt place in haste.

"I'm sorry," said I, "but there's nothing that I can do for you. The ribs are gone under there. They'll set themselves, if you'll give them a fair chance by keeping still for a time. But your friends have left you to take care of yourself, I see."

He cast one glance in the direction in which they had fled. There was not a shadow of resentment in his expression.

"It is the order," said he.

CHAPTER 5

That seems like a rather simple thing to write down, but it gave me an odd feeling as I listened to him, and as I watched him. There was no venom in his manner of saying it.

"But look here, friend," said I, "what will become of you if I leave you out here with a pair of busted ribs, to take care of yourself? Can you stand?"

"I don't know," said he.

"Try."

He stood up like an automaton. He tried a few steps and suddenly sank, gasping, to the ground again. I opened up his coat and his shirt and looked. He was not a very big fellow. A hundred and fifty or sixty pounds, I suppose. He had rushed straight in on the weight of my blow. It was as though a fourteen-pound sledge had been swung with a big man's weight behind it. His side had caved in like the

41

dented part of a paper bag.

I stretched him out and gave him a drink of water and brandy mixed. He accepted it and drank it down. Then he lay quietly, breathing more easily, and watching me with a dull look of wonder. He seemed much more moved by my kindness to him than by the desertion of his companions.

"You're not in shape to take care of yourself out here," I said to him.

He shrugged his shoulders. His movement brought a gasp of pain from him.

"I don't know this part of the country," I went on. "Do you?"

He admitted that he did not. He had simply followed the lead of the others.

"Then you're one of the hired men," said I. "You're not the one with the grudge against Truck Janvers?"

"I don't know who you mean," said he.

It pricked me sharply with anger to hear that sort of baldfaced lie.

"Come, come," said I. "Do you think that I'm a fool? Didn't I see the old fellow lying with the knife in his throat?"

"Was that his name?" said he, as cool as you please.

"Whose name?"

"The name of the man that was killed?"

42

"You didn't know that before?"

"No," said he.

"What the devil!" I cried out at him. "Do you mean to tell me that you went out to slaughter a poor devil whose name you didn't know? You had no grudge against Truck? You didn't even know the name of the old miner in the shack?"

"Sir," said he, "I did not know. However, the knife went straight, did it not?"

"It did," said I, with a shudder.

He smiled and nodded, as pleased as a child.

"You," I shouted, pointing at him in rage and horror, "you threw that knife?"

"Yes, sir."

I choked.

He went on: "I have done much better than that — however. I have thrown just as accurately for a longer distance."

I had to loosen the neckband of my shirt. My blood was turning colder and colder. Yet this man was helpless, and by what he said, I gathered that he considered that he had done nothing really wrong.

"But," he continued as smooth as ever, "it would have been better if I had aimed at your head instead, sir. I remember that there was a wrinkle in your coat just between the shoulder blades. I should have aimed there. It would have been the end!"

I swallowed hard. "I should have lived long enough to put a pair of bullets in you, however," said I.

"Ah, no, sir!" He smiled blandly at me, and he added: "You came out quickly enough even after the other man died."

"Where were you then?"

"Lying close to the ground, just outside the door. Very close to the ground, and spread out so that I could not have done anything to help myself if you had seen me. But I knew that you would not see me. You went out looking man high – not ground high."

This was true enough. I began to see that there was a sort of wit in this cold-blooded devil.

"Friend," said I, "the question is now: What shall I do with you?"

"Leave me, sir, of course," said he.

"To die?"

"It is as God wills," said he with the most perfect indifference. "If He wills that I live, I live; or that I die; and then no man can help me."

"You are ready to be left, then?"

"Certainly, sir."

There was nothing more that I could do for him except to make him a soft bed, and this

I managed by cutting a quantity of branches from the shrubs and piling them out a good two feet thick. It made a spring mattress, fresh and fragrant.

"Lie on this," said I.

He paused to give me one questioning glance, and then he slunk onto the bed. The moment that he touched it, however, he uttered a faint groan of relief and joy and lay motionless for an instant, quivering. I could tell by that, how bitterly the torment must have been wringing him. I suppose that every breath he drew was a torture.

I wrapped him as delicately as I could in my blanket, but in spite of my care he drew a gasping breath or two.

"Now," said I at last, fairly sweating because of the way his pain had gone through me, "do you think that you'll have a fairly comfortable night?"

"Yes, sir."

"Are you warm enough?"

"Ah, my blood is ice!"

I took the saddle blanket and piled it over him. Then I built the fire higher. After that, he told me with a warm, drowsy voice that all was well – that the pain was better – that he would sleep.

But, after a moment, something wakened him.

"You, sir?" he said.

"Well?"

"What blankets remain for you, and what bed?"

I told him that it was not a cold night; and it was not – only nippy. I told him to forget about me and go to sleep. I thought in fact that he had gone to sleep, but after ten minutes I heard him whisper a prayer.

Perhaps it was not his pain that made him say it.

I spent a sufficiently uneasy night. For one thing, it was a bit nippy, and though I could have made myself comfortable enough by building two fires and lying between them, I was not sure enough of my position to take such a measure. I could not tell at what time the remaining pair of the dead man's friends would come snooping back to take a pot shot at me if possible. Though by the manner of their going I felt that they would not hurry back, still, as I have said before, four years of a hunted life give one a stock of natural uneasiness.

When the dawn came, I built up the fire once more and I made it high enough to warm me well. The exercise of tearing out the brush and breaking it off to raise the tower of flames left me perspiring, and I threw off my coat while I cooked a breakfast.

I was in a black humor, with curses just behind the teeth all the time. For here was I nailed down to one spot in the mountains while the quarry to which I had given a week of hard hunting rolled farther and farther from my grasp.

You can imagine what was in my mind when, turning from the fire, I found that that infernal, cold-blooded scoundrel had dared to reach out from his bed, unfurl the coat which I had thrown beside him, and was now busy in examining carefully the contents of the pockets.

I assure you that I was mute and frozen with rage. He was through estimating the contents of the wallet, which was jammed with four thousand dollars in bills of all sizes. That money lay in a ruffled heap in the coat. He was now perusing a deeply creased poster which I had picked up from a crossroad signboard a few days before. I knew what the contents of the poster were. It began with an excellent likeness of the face of Hugo Ames; it went on with an offer of fifteen thousand dollars reward for my apprehension, dead or alive.

I leaned over my captive, quivering. The confounded rascal had the effrontery to smile up in my face. He folded the poster with care, seeing that the creases corresponded with the old ones. Then he extended it to me – still smiling. He picked up my money and began to arrange it once more and restore it to the wallet.

"What in the devil do you mean by it?" I snarled at him.

"What do I mean?" said he, much surprised. "Why, sir, I of course wished to understand you if I could." He paused and then nodded and added: "Now, sir, I understand what happened to Miguel and to me! You are Ames!"

What could one say to a fellow like that? He was not a dumb, dull brute. He simply did not understand things in the light with which they appeared to me and to other people. He had his own way of looking at the world, and it was so different from my way that I concluded it would be foolishness for me to reprimand him or to punish him. One doesn't scold a partly tamed panther.

I was as angry as ever, as I finished cooking the breakfast, which was simple enough, and carried him his food and waited until he had drunk and eaten. For, of course, I had only one cup and one plate. Then I ate my own meal.

"Now that you know my name," said I, "perhaps you'll tell me yours?"

"Surely, sir. I am José."

"José what?" said I.

"I am not a very big man, sir. One name

is enough for me."

I damned him again; this time aloud. Then I went to saddle Spike.

CHAPTER 6

I described a circle about twenty miles in diameter, that day, and I came upon not a sign of a human being! I did not even reach a well-worn trail. In the evening, with Spike tired beneath me, and with myself very tired from the ride and from the sleepless night, I turned back toward the place where I had left José.

I half expected that the other pair would be hidden there, waiting for me. I half hoped that José would be dead from despair, because I had not told him that I was coming back. I had left him my canteen of water and gone off without a word. A good many high-strung people, helpless and deserted in this fashion, would have blown their brains out – and he had a gun, loaded and ready at his hand. That was another provision which I had made without any misgivings or shame.

By this time you can imagine the black frame

of mind when I left him in the morning. But when I came back, there was José, his body still stretched upon the bed of branches. He was smoking a cigarette, and his greeting was characteristic.

"You are late, sir."

"Curse your eyes," said I. "What made you think that I should come back at all?"

"What? Well, one must guess."

"You are a gambler, José," said I. "This time you won. Perhaps tomorrow will be a new day, though."

"Perhaps," said this brazen murderer.

I let him go hungry and thirsty – I saw that the canteen was empty – I even watched him eloquently trying to drain the last drops from it. In the meantime, he had watched my eyes with a look askance. But I refused to understand. I told myself that I should wait until he begged before I gave him any help – if then!

In the meantime, I got out the little trenching shovel which I always carried in my pack. For there is hardly anything – except an ax – so convenient as a shovel when one has to camp out in the mountains in all manner of weather. With that shovel, but even more with my hands, rolling out big rocks, I made a sufficiently deep grave and into it I lowered the body of Miguel. There was the pale shining of

51

a new moon to help me at this grisly work.

When I had finished that necessary task, my head ached and I was thoroughly exhausted. For some of the rocks I had tugged at had been whoppers, and I had put into the labor some of the spite which I felt toward José.

In the meantime, the two who were my quarry were streaking their trail far away from me! Well, it was a desperately trying situation.

I went back and cooked a supper. I had shot a brace of rabbits on my ride, and I roasted them, but when I carried the food to José he took it with a smile and began to maul it in a vague, uninterested way. I noticed closely and saw that he did not swallow a morsel.

"What the devil!" said I. "Have you had a full meal of sunshine?"

"To-day," said the murderer, "José has a religious feeling, and therefore he fasts!"

I cursed him again, with much satisfaction. But on afterthought I remembered the water, and I brought him the filled canteen. The poor rascal drained it to the last drop, hardly lowering it from his lips while he did so.

"It is good," he whispered, and lay with closed eyes in the firelight, still grasping the emptied can.

After that he ate. Literally his throat had been closed with thirst. He ate, and he ate like a wolf. Then I examined the side. It was much swollen and fiery hot to touch. So I bathed it for a long time with cold water.

How much torture he had endured from it during the day and while he ate I cannot say, but I know that as the water began to soothe it and take the inflammation away, he groaned loudly with the great relief.

While I was still bathing it, he slept.

As for me, I was too weary to more than half eat my food, and then, regardless of the perils which might lie in the night for me, I stretched out – heedless of the cold, too, and I slept like a dead man until the direct rays of the sun awakened me. Then I looked about me and considered my work which lay ahead.

It was definite in my mind, now. I could not abandon this injured fellow – even if he were a murderer. He was a human being, and that was all that counted. Strange how much more vital the life in itself becomes when one is in the mountains. One grows to love even the eagle in the air.

That day I made more ample provision for the comfort of José. I made him a fresh bed in a new place – beneath a thicket of small trees about a hundred yards from my first camp – a trebly better place, because a little musical rivulet flowed out from the spring here. Next,

I carried José to the new spot and bedded him down even more thickly than before. There I left him, with plenty of water, and with tobacco, and plenty of cold roast rabbit if he grew hungry in the middle of the day.

I left him looking contentedly up through the branches of the tree at the sky above him, and I started off upon another round to see what I might discover. I struck off due east, traveled a full thirty miles, straight away. But to my consternation, when I came to the end of that distance, I had not found a single sign of a house. Somewhere much nearer than this there must, of course, be the habitation of some men. But I was strange in those mountains, and as I turned Spike back, at noon, I decided that I must give up the attempt.

For, in the meantime, there was no reason for hurrying on. With a two-day start, mounted as they were and now with spare horses to ride from time to time, the companions of José were sure to be vastly beyond my reach. I would need a race of another thousand miles at least to make up for such a handicap.

But it was a bitter sacrifice to make. I reached the camp and found, long before I got to it, a light but husky tenor voice wailing a song before me. It was José, stretched under his tree and whiling away the time with the most perfect good cheer.

He smiled upon me and nodded silently as I appeared.

I, hot from the journey under the sun and hotter still at his sangfroid, could not help breaking out: "Do you know where you are to be taken as soon as your ribs are healed enough to endure traveling?"

"Ah?" said José.

"To the nearest town, where I'll turn you over as the murderer of Truck Janvers."

He considered this for a moment, with the smile still upon his lips.

"You will stay, then, to keep me company in the jail, sir?"

"I'll leave you tied hand and foot in the street at night and with a description of what you've done tied on your neck."

"Ah, sir, will they hang me, then, because of the word of a man who dares not stand before me in the courtroom?"

"Well," said I in a new rage, "I warn you, José, that even if I heal you and turn you loose this time, I'll find a way to get at you later on. I'll find you and the other two, and I'll tie you back to back and burn you over a slow fire – as cowardly assassins like you deserve to die."

"My mother," said he, "once saw a witch burned."

I merely glared at him.

"What do you think that she did when the flames were round her?"

"How should I know, and why should I care?"

He waved my discourtesy aside. "She sang a song – a long song, from the beginning to the end. Then she leaned and breathed deeply of the flames, and she died. Well, sir, it must have been an excellent thing to see. Do you not think so?"

I left him without a word and strode off into the darkness, where I sat down and thanked heaven that I was alone.

Not quite alone. The thought of that black demon pursued me. Yet I did not altogether hate him. He was a camping companion through two days and two nights. Companionship would give certain virtues to Satan himself, I suppose. At least, it does in the mountains.

There is not the slightest use in dwelling over the long and weary days when I remained impatiently with José in the mountains. When he grew better, and reached the time when he could sit up, I had to watch him like a hawk all the time. For I had given him a gun, and I felt that I should be ashamed to take it back from him – as though I could possibly fear a little man whom I had crushed with one stroke of my hand!

A time came when I wished that I had crushed him utterly the first time I encountered him; or else, that I had ridden off on the first morning and left him behind me to die like a fish out of water, or from thirst and the pain of his wound.

I had taken Spike with me every day until, on the sixteenth day of my wait, I took a short hunting trip in the early morning to get a bit of fresh meat for breakfast. I was not gone half an hour before I came back with squirrels. I found that the fire was out and José was not in sight. I called for him, and there was no answer.

Then I yelled for Spike.

And out of the far distance I heard a faintly echoing bray. The infernal scoundrel had stolen the mule and made his get-away!

CHAPTER 7

I felt like a child so angry that it wants to destroy the entire world and furious because it hasn't the strength to do it. I picked up a big rock and smashed it to bits as a way of easing my mind. Then I sat down to consider.

My total possessions consisted of my rifle and two revolvers, together with a very scanty amount of ammunition, because during the days I was taking care of José, I had shot away a good deal of powder and lead to keep us in meat. It takes as much ammunition to kill a squirrel as it does to kill a deer. My mule, and my pack, were now the possessions of the grateful José.

After a time, my anger abated a little. I told myself that I had been simply a fool, and being a fool, I had to take the penalty. Since I had chosen to treat José like a man instead of like a snake, as he deserved, there was nothing for me to do but to dress myself with patience. But, at twenty-two, patience is the smallest of a man's virtues.

Yet, though I was on foot, I had not the slightest idea of giving up the chase. In a few minutes I was up and plugging away on foot. My hope was that José would not understand Spike's uncanny ability to negotiate steep cliffs; and if he kept the mule off the rocks, I still might be able to keep to the trail, whereas if Spike followed the short cuts it would need the eye of an eagle to make out his way.

I kept those hopes all through the morning, for José apparently trusted that no man on foot would attempt to follow a mounted man. But, just before noon, I saw where Spike had lunged over the brow of the mountain and shortened the trail by going down into the valley beneath. I knew that I was close to the end of my trailing.

Indeed, within a single hour the sign was lost. José, apparently seeing at once the peculiar talents of the mule, had pushed him straight ahead at every tangle of rock and was following an air-line course across the country. There among the rocks I lost the sign and sat down to think over what more I might be able to do. Finally I decided that I should try to cut for the sign of the four horses and their two riders, but I had no luck whatever!

I went back to the direction in which Spike had been traveling and I tried to lay a straight course across country in the general trend which José had been following. The quartet had been using the easier ways of getting across the land, but José, on Spike, used him as an eagle uses its wings. I was fairly confident that he had picked out the exact direction.

So I laid out a landmark to the north and west and another to the south and east, exactly on the course which José had been following. For five long days, I pushed the leagues behind me.

On the fifth day I dropped from the upper mountains into a little valley and saw, to my great delight, half a dozen ranch houses scattered here and there. Best of all, I saw some horses and I felt that the end of my long trek on foot had come. This was worth a pause. I wanted a horse, but I wanted one able to carry two hundred and twenty pounds and carry it fast and far.

I found a tiny bit of freckled boyhood under the shadow of a great straw sombrero. He sat on a pot-bellied old pony – a caricature of age and weakness with that infant holding the reins. I spoke to him.

"Sammy, whereabouts is there a good horse for sale?"

Sammy looked me over with care and a fearless eye. There was a good deal to see. I had broken my razor six weeks before. There was already a considerable forest on my face before I started on this trail, and now my features were well hidden.

"Pa has a couple of hosses to sell," he declared at last. "Hey, Spot, you old fool!"

He cracked his blacksnake in the air. He was riding herd on a score of milk cows and heifers, to keep them on a stretch of pasture and away from a field of sowed barley hay.

"They're too wore out for cutting wood," said the boy. "Maybe they'd suit you, though."

"A good horse, son," I repeated, "that can carry me and carry me fast."

He looked over my bulk and then grinned. "Old Brinsly, he got up half a dozen of the San Marin hosses a while back," said the boy. "Maybe you'd want to pay the price of one of them?"

The name stuck in my throat. San Marin! I remembered where I had last seen it.

"What are the San Marin horses?" I asked him.

"Ain't you heard? They're the brood of that Comanche hoss. Pa says they can't be beat. But the price of 'em can't be beat, neither. Nothing less than five hundred. That's all they want!"

"I'd like to look at them for fun," said I. "Where's the Brinsly place?"

He pointed it out to me – a wedge of roof rising out of the horizon mist, and I started off to see the Comanche horses. It was a stiff five-mile walk to the place, but I had my reward. The very first pasture into which I looked contained six horses of a build which I thought I recognized. I had seen that cut of horse between me and the dawn colors some twenty days before – horses that seemed half Arab and half thoroughbred!

They were all bay and chestnut – the colors of hot blood, and they were made according to a style that filled the eye. They were not big – I suppose that the tallest of them was not two inches over fifteen hands – but I did not have to ask if they could carry weight. What quarters, what shoulders, what powerful short coupling! I suppose that to some they would have seemed a little short of leg – rather pony built. But I noticed the fine taper from haunch to hock, and I told myself that this was running stock. I like a horse with brains, too, and these animals had intelligence. They looked back at me out of their deerlike eyes.

I went to the house and asked the cook for Mr. Brinsly.

"What for?" said he.

through the rest of my journey, Sandy
ked like a trooper. She reeled off her fifty
s a day through all manner of going. On
eleventh day after I had left Mr. Brinsly's
e, I worked Sandy up a steep mountain-
and saw directly beneath me the beautiful
y which bore the name of San Marin.

"I want to buy one of his San Marin horses,"
said I.

It made his jaw drop and presently, after he
had hurried back into the house, a thin-faced
man of middle-age with the look and the voice
of a gentleman, came out to me.

He did not show his surprise or his curiosity
at the sight of me. He merely said: "I'm sorry
but these horses of mine are not for sale. I
brought them up here at a considerable expense
and great cost of trouble."

But what I noticed most of all was that he
did not look at me as I was accustomed to have
people look. He did not stare at me with the
words "Hugo Ames" forming on his lips. I saw
that I could thank my broken razor of six weeks
before. So I told him frankly my trouble was,
that my weight broke down an average horse
and that I saw his San Marin stock looked like
weight carriers.

He took me out to the pasture, at that, and
he seemed glad enough to talk about them. It
was his hope, he told me, to gradually breed
them until they had replaced all the common
stock on his ranch, and he pointed them out
to me one by one until his finger stopped with
a low-built chestnut mare.

"I could let you have her," said he. "Except
that I would not sell her to any man. There is

too much devil in her. I even hesitate about breeding her, for the fiend which was in Comanche is in her, full stock!"

I looked at her again. She was not as pretty as the others, but her ample and powerful lines appealed to me. I asked him his price. As for her temper, I did not care for that. It is my theory that no horse is bad because of wrong instincts, but simply because it has been maltreated by people. I felt there was plenty of time for me to tame Sandy, as he called her. So I asked him to name a price, and he put on a high one – seven hundred and fifty dollars.

She was driven into the corral and I looked her over – perfectly sound, six years old, in the maturity of her strength, and with a wicked eye that promised a bad temper, to be sure, but the endurance which a great many mean horses possess. I paid Mr. Brinsly his seven hundred and fifty and bought an old saddle and bridle from him also. Then I inquired about San Marin and told him that I had come down from the north.

There was still a long journey ahead of me. Five hundred miles, according to Brinsly.

But that distance did not daunt me. I was more and more convinced that this was exactly the type of horse which I had seen ridden by the four whom I had trailed, so I started

down the road with Sandy on a l[...] hind me, to the great disappoint[...] Brinsly, who had expected me to [...] at once.

I had not such pride, however. [...] as well as most men, but I am no [...] saddle. I decided that when I mo[...] I would have her more or less a[...]

What I did, then, was to stop [...] and load her with a heavy pack [...] great many unnecessaries in the li[...] goods which would increase her [...] the pack. Then I took Sandy strai[...] a two-day march. I gave her sca[...] food or for water, and I walke[...] heaviest going that I could find[...]

At the end of the second da[...] was quite downheaded with wea[...] strapped the pack and I risked [...] saddle. It was exactly as I had [...] might be. Sandy snorted and trie[...] jumps in the thick sand, which [...] that I had selected. Then she s[...] flattened her ears. I slapped her [...] flank with my open hand, and Sar[...] a gentle trot.

I was delighted; my delight w[...] mature, but that, however, is son[...] I must tell about later on. From [...]

CHAPTER 8

It was one of those places which appear too good by far to be true. There were not even any high mountains near it to roughen its outlook. All the higher, sterner peaks stood back at a distance where the horizon blue would soften them. Beneath them were smoother heights covered with a great foresting of pines and of other evergreens, and below these again, were gently rolling hills covered with pasture lands that stretched down to the bottom of the valley where the San Marin curved back and forth among the green fields of alfalfa and through orchards and vineyards.

It was the very perfection of quiet beauty, that landscape, and in the midst of it, stretched out irregularly, with an arm thrown across the Marin by means of a bridge and another village on the farther bank, was the town itself. All the walls, from this distance, were purest white, and the roofs were varying shades from pink to red. I could see the plazas, and the little green shadings which mean garden places and groups of shade trees. I could see the streets, white with dust.

This was the hot hour of the day, and there was no life in the valley, no life in the town to meet the eye. It was the time of siesta, religiously kept. I had to shake my head with force in order to remember that this was a part of our United States and not a section out of old Mexico.

By the time that Sandy had taken me down to the town, the valley was waking. I passed half a dozen great-wheeled carts, which had presumably taken vegetables into the town in the morning and were now returning empty. The drivers were a jolly lot. All of them pointed with astonishment to me and then to the fine mare which I was riding. No doubt the contrast was weird enough.

When I came closer to the place a flashing fellow rode out past me. He was like a thing out of a picture book with the wind flapping his gaudy Mexican sombrero and the sun rippling and splashing on the gold and silver laces that covered his Mexican short jacket. He was not a youth, but a fellow with a face half dignified and half villainous, garnished with an angular beard and waxed mustaches. He would have passed me without a look, but his glance touched on Sandy and then he was surprised into an exclamation of extreme wonder.

For, in fact, he was himself riding upon a horse of the same breed, but of lines much inferior to those of my mare. I began to wonder that I had never heard of the breed until so recently. Evidently this little valley was filled with that Comanche blood. However, it is true that in the West there are a thousand odd nooks and corners cut off from the knowledge of the rest of the world by barriers of desert and mountains, as San Marin was cut off.

The streets were typical of those of any second- or third-rate Mexican town. They were fetlock deep in liquid dust except for occasional cobbled stretches. Children played in that sea of white, and pigs grunted through it and refused to budge for a passing rider. In the deep, cool shadows of the low doorways, sat squat women who shouted gossip to one another. Or in the dim interiors, they were patting out tortillas. Spicy fragrance of peppers sifted through the air. On the whole, there was a sense of pleasant life – lazy life – contented life.

I found the barber in front of his shop, talking to the shoemaker, who was working a soft dressing into a great stiff square of leather in the sunshine. They, like the others, stopped their talk and stared at me and gaped at my horse, as though they knew perfectly well that it was a seven-hundred-and-fifty-dollar purchase, and that a man who looked like a tramp had very little right to be sitting in the saddle. However, I had made up my mind as to what I must do. The flash of the splendid gentleman who had passed me as I entered the town had filled me with an inspiration.

When I sat in the barber's chair I did not need to be told to use Spanish on the barber. I gave him careful directions in that tongue. I had been away on a long hunting trip. I had been ill. Now I wished to be trimmed up. I would not have him shave me all over. Instead, I had him leave a short beard, trimmed to a dangerous point, and I had him leave mustaches. They were not long enough to draw out too fine, but they made a black shadow across my upper lip. Then I had my hair trimmed also – not too short. When all was ended I called for a mirror and regarded myself.

It was a notable transformation. Even the wide, short nose had gained an indefinable touch of elegance. I was at a step one of the pseudo-aristocrats, and I had to bite my lip to keep from smiling. With a lace collar around my neck, I might have stepped into the frame of a seventeenth-century painting. There was an odd up-angling of my eyebrows which the barber did not need to assist. It was there by nature – something not noticeable before, but now, added to the mustache and to the beard, it gave a little sinister air which was perfectly in keeping with the part which I wished to fill.

I paid the barber liberally and then went to a clothing store. I came in a hobo, barbered to the taste of a grandee. I went out a harmonious picture. I came in a sober citizen. I came out a golden flash. I stood on the steps of the store and pushed the heavy sombrero back from my head, and as I rolled a cigarette, I was aware of my brilliance in the sloping sun of the afternoon. Others were aware, also. A youngster driving a dusty herd of milk cows home, rolled his eyes at me in awe. A pair of girls, with baskets in their hands, stopped for a single flash of me and then hurried on, whispering together.

I fancied myself very much in this new toggery and this new style of hair-on-the-face. Then I went to the saddlery and outfitted Sandy with saddle and bridle after the most fashionable style in San Marin. When she carried me down the street after that, I could not help feeling that the silly little fool was arching her neck partly because of the little tinkling of bells at her throat latch, and partly because she was really proud to have such a splendid rider on her back!

Next I went to the hotel and asked for a room. Oh, there was no doubt as to the effect which I made. I was implored to inscribe my name upon the register. It was done. I was begged to step up after the proprietor. He walked sidewise in front of me like a crab — for fear he should insult me by turning his back! I felt that it was my duty to find fault. He showed me three rooms. I declared that none of them were fit to stable my horse in. While he stood perspiring and rubbing his anxious hands together, I told him that I would take the corner room.

"Señor Mendez," said he, "we shall do our best to make you happy here."

Yes, I have forgotten to say that I had written upon the register: "Francisco Mendez."

So I stolled down the stairs again, and stood on the veranda airing myself and smoking a tailor-made cigarette, and yearning mightily in my heart for a sack of tobacco and brown papers!

Well, I was wonderfully happy. Stolen happiness I felt that it was, and therefore doubly and trebly sweet to me. But consider that during several years I had not shown myself to other men except for a fleeting glimpse, gun in hand.

Now, however, I could look others boldly in the face, secure in the belief that they would never recognize me, for my mustache and the pointed beard added a good eight years to my age. I was a full thirty years or more in appearance. The only danger was my voice and my bulk which was a good deal greater than that of most men. But the long tramp had thinned my face, and I determined that it would be kept thin. The pointed beard masked the blunt, heavy lines of my jaw. I felt that I had left behind me somewhere among the rude mountains the ghost of Hugo Ames upon whose head lay the burden of a fifteen-thousand-dollar reward if he were apprehended alive or dead. There remained only a new self, resplendent and without fear of what the eyes of other men might see in me.

But ah, how marvelous it was to bathe in the presence of other men. I felt a great expanding of the heart. At the thought of returning again to the lonely and the dreary life, my soul grew small and cold.

A cowpuncher, inevitably American in his rolling gait and his rough clothes, turned in from the street and swallowed a grin as he saw me.

"Hot as the devil, ain't it, partner?" said he

with great good nature.

"Have little English, señor," said I, and looked blankly down upon him.

He nodded and joined another man on the veranda of the old building – a prospector by the weedy look of him and the palms of his hands, whitened with calluses.

"By the cut of him," said the puncher, speaking freely in the English which it was presumed I did not understand, "by the cut of him, I figgered that he might be quite a man. But doggone me if he ain't just greaser plain and simple."

"Not so simple as that," said the other.

"Two hundred pounds," said one.

"And thirty!" said the other.

"Maybe you're right. But him bein' a greaser, you or me could handle him, I guess."

I bit my lip, and thus eradicated the smile. This was typical Western thinking on their part, and I sympathized with it. I shouted for a *mozo*, and when a boy came panting out to me, I pointed out the best and largest chair and told him that it was too small and ordered another from the interior. He scampered away and presently he came back with a leather easy chair. Still it would not do. I pointed out some imaginary dust, and when that was removed, I deigned to stretch myself at ease.

There was a muffled snort from the prospector. "Too fine to live outside of cotton batting!"

What the reply was I did not know; for, at that instant, I was lost to all other sights and all other sounds except the trampling of a small cavalcade of horses and, in the midst of them the familiar face of José!

CHAPTER 9

I carried no guns for exterior show, in this fine
new costume of mine, but I made an instinctive gesture with my hands toward a pair of
weapons which were ready beneath the clothes.
Then I controlled my impulse. There was no
need of making a fool of myself. I could not
remedy matters by shooting a man in the streets
of San Marin. For the root of the matter which
I wished to discover lay not in the death of José
– that was only a personal spite of my own –
it consisted in discovering the reason for the
slaying of Truck Janvers.

Besides, there was enough for me to look at.
José was one of a cavalcade of four riders, all
mounted upon fine horses of the Comanche
breed, and in front of them, not riding even
these beautiful animals, but mounted upon true
thoroughbreds of the finest stock, rode as pretty a girl as I had ever seen – a beauty of the

highest Spanish type, with all her dark loveliness excellently set off by the golden-haired cavalier who accompanied her.

Yes, they made as handsome a couple as I ever laid eyes on. They passed on, chatting and laughing together. I watched them out of sight, with the dust cloud curling up behind their grim escort. Then I called for a boy again, and the *mozo* was instantly before me.

"Who has just passed?" I asked.

He did not have to ask what I meant. Apparently all eyes in San Marin had been focused upon this brilliant train.

"It is Señorita Caporno and her men, and Señor Vidett rode with her."

"Who is Señorita Caporno? Who is Señor Vidett?"

For, I said to myself, one of the pair was the cause of the dastardly murder of Truck Janvers. One of the pair had sent four hired killers far north to find and to destroy him. I swallowed my anger. My eagerness was greater still than the heat in my blood.

"The Señor Caporno –" began the boy.

"Is there a Señor Caporno?"

"Ah, señor! Have you not heard of him?"

"Never," I admitted.

"But he was a president –"

"A president?"

"Ah, of a great country, señor!"

"Send out the master," I said to him. "I wish to hear of these people."

The proprietor came out at once, smiling and obsequious. I felt that it was my duty still, to treat him as if he were dirt beneath my feet. How to step out of the lofty role which I had created for myself, I did not know.

"The valley is not a complete desert," said I. "I have seen one flower in it, señor."

"True, true!" said he. "You have seen the señorita."

"Caporno. Is not that the name?"

"That is the name. But did the *mozo* tell you right? Is it possible, señor, that you have not heard of –"

"Of her husband?"

"Husband? Her father, señor! He was president of Venzago."

"I have never heard of him. Are they passing through the valley?"

"By the blessing of heaven, they have favored the valley by coming to live here! If the señor would trouble himself to rise – yonder – between the two houses – he will see their estate – like a king's palace, señor. For the wealth of Señor Caporno is the wealth of a king! For two years, I cannot tell you how many scores of men worked to build it.

"First all the sand was dug away, and then the earth beneath, and then they came to the sandstone, and they cut through that, and still, beneath the sandstone, there was an ocean of solid black rock. Even in that they blasted and drilled, as though they were making a mine. I and all the other people in San Marin went every Sunday to look. It was a great hole in the ground! You could have poured all of the town into it, I think!

" 'What is it for?' we said to one another.

"Then we saw chambers being cut and squared. Was it to be a house under the ground? No, for then masons came and walls of stone were raised – so thick as this! My arms could not span them. The great walls rose and rose to a good height. Señor, will you believe that that mighty work which we saw, it was no more than the digging of cellars for the house which was to be built? For two years they dug and they built. At last it was finished. And there it stands! Through the trees, you cannot guess. But it is very grand!"

It looked very grand, just as he said. About all that I could see beyond the foresting of palms and trees was an occasional glimpse of a white façade, and a long stretching roof line.

But what took root in my heart was: How could any man or woman living in such a palace as this desire to compass the death of an obscure prospector, a lonely, rough, friendly and harmless old man like Truck Janvers? It seemed to me that once more I heard the knife strike home in the hollow of the throat of Truck. No matter what the contrast of ideas might be, I decided that I would never rest until I had got to the bottom of the trouble. But, in the meantime, I asked for more news concerning the proprietor of that estate. I got what I wanted.

The business of the hotel could wait, now that the proprietor had such a story to tell. I suppose that he felt it almost too good to be true — that he should find a stranger who really was unaware of the history of Manuel Caporno.

Manuel Caporno, I learned, had been an obscure shopkeeper in the little South American republic of which he was a citizen. He had come to maturity without distinguishing himself, and for some years after that he still advanced only in wealth. For Señor Caporno was one of those shrewd weather prophets who can tell when a Latin-American revolution is pending, and also which side is apt to win. He knew with extraordinary precision just when it was better to lie low and let the government carry on. He knew, also, when the revolting party had a good chance of winning.

Then, like a good businessman, he advanced a quantity of much-needed cash and took, in return, from the rebel leaders paper promises worth three times the sum he had advanced. This was high gambling, but Señor Caporno consistently won. The handicap was not too great for his astute wits. When the rebels went into office, he cashed in the paper promises and took home a cartload of loot, almost literally, although his hand was not seen in the revolt itself.

So that when the party which was down wished to come up again, he was ready, if their chances seemed good, to back them as he had backed the last comers. He even did more than this. He discovered that the business of revolutions was so profitable that they should be encouraged. And he found a way of encouraging them most effectually.

The genial Caporno found that, in that small country of his, the lack of machine guns and fine rifles usually beat the losing side. And, when he saw the storm of revolt beginning to lower over the distant horizon, he sent abroad and would purchase a whole cargo of ammunition and guns of all kinds. He chartered a big steamship and brought this cargo to his native shores.

When the proper signal was given, the revolt

began. Five thousand unarmed men suddenly rushed to the place where the ship was waiting. Their hands were filled with guns, their belts with ammunition. A barefoot trio of beggars suddenly became an "army" and the transformation was so sudden, the danger appeared so quickly and so near to the capitol whose possession usually decided the fate of the revolution, that on three separate occasions Señor Caporno became the master of the fortunes of his country at a single stroke.

He himself remained in the background. All that he took was not honor, but a very sizable proportion of the loot. When he had the money, he invested it discreetly in gilt-edged foreign bonds – American preferred! At length, however, having served both parties many times, he fell into disrepute with both. A little comparing of notes made the leaders on both sides feel that Caporno had played the traitor to both. Accordingly, he was suddenly proscribed.

Across the mouth of the river which communicated with the capital, the republic's two little gunboats were stationed to keep off any new shiploads of arms and conserve the peace of the nations.

However, they did not reckon upon the brains of the amiable Caporno. Whereas upon the one hand he had furnished new arms in every war, on the other hand he had made it a point to buy in the old arms which were for sale for the price of a few drinks of native brandy as soon as the revolution was over. In the cellars of his great house there was a perfect arsenal, which had gradually accumulated.

Now that his head was in danger, he played his ace and suddenly appeared in the field as the representative of "business" – a man who wished to do away with revolutions, one who appealed to the common sense and the common wallets of all the shopping and trading classes of the republic. Down with the military! was his cry. Away with the professional soldiers!

He was heard and he was believed. The well-to-do mustered their allies and their servants and their friends. The rude mob was equipped by magic from the cellars of the great house of Caporno. The colonel who rode with a squadron to arrest the "traitor" was arrested in turn and hanged to a tree with his warrant tied about his neck.

His men, of course, readily joined the ranks of the new "president." Caporno marched straight upon the capitol. There was a random skirmish in its vicinity and there the money-lender showed that he had courage as well as business acumen for, in the middle of the fight, he rallied a stanch body of clerks and shop-keepers and drove straight at the center of the enemy. The enemy's center was not broken, however. For they ran so fast that the men of Caporno never came up with them. In this manner Caporno became president.

It was soon seen, however, that Caporno was in fact even more of a businessman than the country had bargained for. He knew exactly how much in taxes could be gathered and how little must be spent to run the administration. The difference between the two sums he placed in his own pocket – or, rather, in a treasury fund which he declared was to accumulate to pay off the national debts.

He bought in a great many of the govern-ment bonds – which were not worth a great deal more than the paper they were printed on – and on the strength of the "debt fund" the bonds leaped up to almost half of their face value. Whereupon he unloaded his holdings and put away in foreign securities another com-fortable fortune.

This was not all, however. Señor Caporno's heavy taxes began to cause murmurs, and the traders and the shopkeepers were the first to wail, because he knew their status so exactly that he understood just how deep their pockets were. A new revolution began to gather upon the cloudy horizon. It concluded in a secret march by night of several thousand angry men. They reached the splendid house of Señor Caporno – and they were paralyzed with astonishment to find that it no longer belonged to their president. He had sold it only the day before to a rich Englishman who coveted its wide lawns and its cool shade trees. They began to search for their president. And, among other places, they looked in the government treasury. There they did not find him.

Neither did they find the "debt fund." It had disappeared, and at the same time a little gasoline yacht was sliding down the river and making excellent time toward the open sea with the "business" president on board and his daughter sitting with him upon the deck. And so it was, eventually, that he looked around until he discovered the valley of San Marin. There he had settled down.

I wondered at the narrator even more than at his narration. For when he finished, he exclaimed: "Ah, yes, he is a brave man, a wise man, a great man, the Señor Caporno!"

"But a bit of a rascal?" I could not help suggesting.

"Rascal? Señor! That is a strange thing to say."

CHAPTER 10

That was a terse way of saying that when vice reached to a certain altitude, it is no longer vice, but victory! I, however, was remembering Truck Janvers, who had been murdered in his wretched little shack. What possible connection there could be between the splendid ex-president of Venzago and old Janvers I could not imagine. But I was prepared to find out.

It was dusk when the proprietor finished this long tale about the exile from Venzago, whose crimes were too beautifully successful and polished to be called crimes. My mind was so full of the story that I went out to walk for a while through the quieting street in the evening and to enjoy the cool of the day. But, going down the steps, my spur unluckily caught on the top of the veranda and I stumbled down and ran heavily into my pair of Americans — the cowpuncher and the prospector. They had

had their share of tequila that afternoon, and tequila is famous for making a man savage. It was the prospector whom I had lunged against. He turned with a snarl.

"The greaser dude!" he gasped, and smote fairly for my jaw.

I stepped back from the wind of his fist and as I did so the cowpuncher leaped in. I was in perfect balance to duck, and I did, and struck low and hard at the same moment. Exactly as that unlucky José had thrown his weight against my driving fist, so the cowpuncher came against it. Exactly as the ribs of José had been broken, so I felt the side of the puncher yield beneath my driving knuckles. He fell with a gasp of agony.

The prospector with one startled glance at me forgot all about fighting and leaned over his stricken friend. Between us we carried him up to the porch of the veranda and sent for a doctor. To him I explained in good Spanish just what had happened. I told him, moreover, that the ribs would not be well instantly, and I suggested that the patient be kept at the hotel at my expense.

All of this was done. They carried the cowpuncher into a comfortable room, and I left him with a great swathing of tape around his middle. The prospector met me in the hall.

He said in fairly good Spanish: "My friend and I made a mistake. A hard mistake to make!"

He grinned at me. I wanted to grin back. Instead, I assured him that I would take care of his companion until he was well. It was a great relief to the miner. I suppose that his own stock of money was running low; in fact, the next morning he was gone.

That night I slept as a man sleeps who has long been away from beds – four years away from them, and in all that time the nearest I had come to one had been ten nights on a prison cot! It was broad morning when I opened my eyes, and for a moment a wave of confused fears rushed over me, for I felt as though I were back in jail once more – so unfamiliar to me was anything more confining than the open sky above my head. When I had my wits about me once more, I went down to breakfast and then out toward the veranda. In the doorway I paused, for just across the street, his eyes fastened full upon me, was José!

He sat his saddle motionless, and motionless were his bright eyes on my face. But, after the first shock, the first impulse to draw and to shoot, I stepped calmly out on the veranda and took a chair for my morning cigarette. There I sat and smoked it, apparently indifferent to the questing eyes of the rider across the street.

Presently, as though he had made up his mind, he touched his horse with the spurs and they were off down the street with hoofbeats silenced in the velvet of the dust. It left me with a mind spinning in doubts.

Obviously José had taken up his post that morning for the sake of a glimpse of me. I was not long in finding a reason for it. No doubt his own ribs were still sore from the blow I had given them. If the story came to his ears of how a big stranger in San Marin had crushed the side of another man, it would not have been odd if he had wished to make sure that the stranger and Hugo Ames were not the same man. What the impertinent rascal had decided I, of course, could not imagine. But I was fairly convinced that he could not have pierced through my disguise. Not, at least, from such a distance as across the street when I, standing before a mirror, hardly could recognize my own face!

Yet I was uneasy. I knew the shrewdness of that fellow from of old. First of all, I cursed the weight of my hand. Moreover, I felt the incongruity of a Mexican dandy striking a blow as hard as a pugilist. That would need some explaining!

Altogether, I was thoroughly uncomfortable.

I lingered on the veranda for some time, hardly knowing what to think, and uneasily scanning the street, up and down – half expecting that, at any moment, a sheriff with a posse behind him might ride into view and come up to arrest me under the name of Hugo Ames.

But the next thing of interest that I saw was, an hour later, one of the unmistakable riders of Caporno, tall, slender, lean of face, and mounted on a horse of the Comanche breed that floated along with a swinging gallop like a swallow on the wing.

He came up to the hotel, dismounted, and then advanced straight upon me. He took off his hat to speak to me.

"You," said he, "are Señor Mendez?"

"I am," said I.

"I bring you a letter from Señor Caporno," said he.

I ripped open the envelope and took out a sheet of stiff linen paper. Upon it, in a shapeless, sprawling hand was written, in Spanish:

Señor Mendez: We have heard of you, and heard of you in such a way that I am making bold to send a letter without a proper introduction. Whatever you may think of this brusque behavior, I entreat you to make allowances. In a word, Señor

Mendez, I have learned that with your fist you break the side of a strong man as though his ribs were deadwood.

I, señor, am in a position in which I need very much the help of a man who, I think, may be your very self. Now, this may seem to you like the offer of a position. But, in all seriousness, whether you are open to such offers or not, it would be a great pleasure to me to meet you and talk with you.

As I am at present confined to my chair with a touch of illness, I am bold to beg you to visit me at your pleasure during the day.

Forgive me for this unconventional approach and believe me, obediently yours,

Manuel Caporno

Now, when I had finished this letter, I straightway turned back to the beginning of it and read it through again, and then folded it slowly and restored it to the envelope, and placed the envelope carefully inside my coat pocket.

The possibilities were simply infinite! I, having trailed my four wild riders to the south, had at last come upon them near their lair. To that lair I was now being freely invited! It was such good fortune that I could not help but doubt it. Even the worst of fools would have done so. It might be that the intentions of Señor Caporno were the highest and the best in the world.

But then again, if the sharp eye of José had detected me under my disguise, might it not be that I was being invited to the great house of Caporno so that a too inquisitive trailer might be taken off the scent?

How taken off? I remembered the knife which had slid into the throat of Truck Janvers. Perhaps he, too, had mysteriously been put in a position to ask too many questions.

Then I stole a glance at the face of the rider and discovered that he was looking me over with a sort of childish admiration which centered upon my brawny hands. I wondered, suddenly, how those big, broad, sun-blackened hands of mine fitted in with the clothes and the mannerisms of a Mexican gentleman of leisure? I saw that, according to the circumstances in which I found myself, I should have to be prepared to play a variety of roles. In a word, I should have to expand my character to meet varying needs.

With all of this in mind, I found at last that the temptation to beard the lion in his den was altogether too much for me. I got up suddenly and told the rider that I should accompany him to the house of Caporno. At this, he bowed with much ceremony. I could not help admiring Caporno, in the first instance, for the skill with which he had disciplined the members of his household staff. A discipline so perfect, indeed, that he was enabled to send them a thousand miles to kill a man and they performed his orders with the most astonishing skill and celerity. I had no doubt that their reward was no more than a single added month's pay. A good shopkeeper like Caporno was not one to waste money right and left!

I had the stable boys saddle Sandy for me, and when the mare was brought around to the front of the hotel, burnished and shining from a most scrupulous grooming, I leaped into the saddle and we started down the street. I began to ask a question of my companion, but I found that he had fallen back a length to the rear, and when I shortened rein to let him come up with me, he slowed his own horse to a corresponding degree. This was his manner, therefore, of accompanying a superior. So I loosed the reins of Sandy and gave up the idea of pumping any worthwhile information out of him. I would have to trust to eyes and ears to read the character of the house and the people in it after I got there.

We turned presently from the main road — the voice of the rider directing me — and we entered a winding avenue with a lofty bordering of palms upon either side. This guided us up a gentle elevation and at length brought us before the long, white face of the house of Caporno. There were few trees near the house. They would have marred the lines of its simple beauty. But big trees in the distance were piled up to make a background, and all between the walls and the forestation stretched green lawns and delicately designed gardens.

When I dismounted from my horse, I felt that I was indeed visiting royalty. One servant took my reins; I could not help wondering if I should ever see Sandy again as a second servant met me and escorted me over the broad steps, and into the mouth of the patio. There, in the coolness of the colonnade, I had my first sight of that great man, Manuel Caporno.

CHAPTER 11

One expects adventurers and political climbers to be lean and hungry men, according to Shakespeare's prescription for them. Caporno was not of that type. Having seen his daughter, I expected to find a handsome fellow, slender-featured, gray of head, cool and distinguished in his manner and in his appearance.

I was utterly wrong.

I saw a fat man lying in a great easy chair which must have been built to order to accommodate his bulk. I saw a throat which was a loose mass of rolling flesh, and above that throat a face very broad at the jowls, garnished with a huge arched nose and a pair of bright eyes, and to crown all, a sloping, narrow forehead. I saw, to match that forehead, small, white, fat hands and one foot clad in a very small shoe – femininely small. The other foot, swathed in flannel bandages, lay upon a cushioned stool.

This bulky fellow had a table upon either side of him. On the one was a heap of books. On the other was an arrangement of silver pitchers, frosted with dim ice on the outside. And there were glasses, and ice heaped in other silver dishes — ice chipped neatly into cubes.

He waved to me from a distance, as if I were an old friend.

"Hush!" said he. "Walk softly, Mendez!"

An odd greeting for a stranger.

But one did not think of disobeying Caporno. I softly stepped quietly forward and found his fat arm rigid in pointing.

"Look! The beauty!" said he.

A great blue jay was standing on the marble rim of the fountain bowl in the center of the patio garden. Now and then he let his body dip forward so that the crystal spray showered over him. Then he flaunted the water off with a jerk of his wings. The sun, shining upon his water-cleaned feathers, made him as brilliant as a jewel. Suddenly he spread his wings and darted off into the air.

Caporno was stricken with grief. "Ah, ah!" said he. "There is a joy flown out of my life forever. Call him back, Pedro! Call him back, thin devil!"

A little man stepped from the shadow next to the wall. I had not noticed him before. He was part Indian, I thought. He had the face of a philosopher, and above it a crown of perfectly white hair. His skin had been grayed by time. It seemed to be coated with dust. He was a very erect little man, wonderfully thin, but not unhealthy in appearance. I saw that he was old, very, very old. I thought that I had never seen so old a man. Yet, at the first glance, he appeared anything but that. There was hardly a wrinkle in his face!

Pedro, as he came in answer to the voice of his master, paused just behind the chair.

"I have not understood how to talk to a bird – since fifty years, señor," said he.

"You – ha? Not for fifty years?"

Caporno whistled and then glanced aside at me with a shrewd look.

"An old scoundrel, Mendez, you see?"

Of course, there was no answer to make to such a question; I did not attempt one.

"Sit down," said Caporno. "Pedro, why is there not a chair? I told you the gentleman would come to see me!"

"Not until this afternoon," said Pedro, without changing his expression.

He spoke to what was apparently an empty door, but instantly a *mozo* appeared from the house and placed a chair for me.

"So here we are, but we have not touched hands."

He stretched a fat palm to me. I took it. It was like handling a thing not of flesh, for there was no warmth in it.

"What will you drink?" said he, as I sat down. "Whisky?"

I shook my head.

"Wine, then?" murmured he approvingly. He waved his hand at the liberal store of liquids on the table.

"I shall not drink," I told him.

"Ah, señor," said he sadly. "Are you one of those who have caught the terrible American habit? You drink nothing?"

"Not," said I, "when I talk to Señor Caporno."

He glanced sharply aside at this, reading me, and reading me not covertly, but openly, his thought showing in his eyes. Then he began to smile. His great loose throat began to quiver, and the smile proceeded to a chuckle. The chuckle deepened to laughter; the laughter spread and extended to a terrific gale of mirth which roared like thunder up and down the patio and sent crowding echoes back against my ears.

The laughter ended with a screech, and he made a futile grasp at his swathed foot. Then he lay stiffly back in his chair, moaning and groaning and wriggling his finger in the air, and twisting his face into a thousand contortions.

"Oh, Lord! Oh, Lord!" cried Caporno. "What pain! What exquisite pain. Through the whole soul! My whole soul is now in my foot! Pedro!"

Pedro did not move from the shadow against the wall.

"Pedro!"

"Señor?"

"Will not purgatory fire be like this?"

"Hell fire, señor," said Pedro.

There was a gasp from Caporno, and he twisted in his chair as though about to rise and put his hands on the old man. However, that sudden movement seemed to bring back the twinge, and he lay gasping and groaning for another moment, his eyes closed.

"You are going to be bad for my gout, Mendez!" he said at last. "I see that you are going to be bad as the devil for my gout. Ah, ah!"

The last two groans seemed to banish every vestige of his pain, and he shrugged himself into a more erect position in his chair.

"Now I can be sure of at least one half hour of comfort," said he. "Gout and I arrange truces between our battles. We never break the truces. Never! There was a time when I played the man and refused to make a sound. I have smiled and talked small talk to pretty fools of women while the gout was rending me. I have risen, Mendez, and danced divinely with them, while my foot was a burning mass of fire! But I have learned! Gout is a devil. It torments me until I scream. But when it hears me cry out, it knows that it has done very well. So I cry just as loud as the pain is. Sometimes I scream like a woman. Do I not, Pedro?"

"Oh, like a puma, señor," said the old man.

At this pointed rejoinder I half expected that my host would break into a furious exclamation, but he did not seem to hear.

"Screaming will rout the gout quicker than anything else," said Caporno. "What is it that you would have to drink?"

"Water, Señor Caporno."

"Oh, well, you are wise. Only a very great fool drinks when he talks with me. I, however, drink constantly, and upon all occasions. There is no moment that is not improved by liquor – if one can afford it. If one can afford it!"

He repeated that last idea, nodding and blinking and smiling to himself.

As I write down what this man did, I feel as if I were describing a beast. As a matter of fact, he was not exactly repulsive. I thought that he was a great deal of a pig. I thought also that he was a great deal of a man.

"Wine, Pedro!" he snapped. "Cold wine. Ice cold. I am hot at present from laughing and screaming."

He looked askance at me. "The laughing was your fault, Mendez. I shall not forgive!"

He wagged his finger at me. "Now," said he, "when are you coming to live with me?"

It astounded me, as of course he intended that it should.

"It is a question of which I have not thought," said I.

"It is a question of which you *have* thought," said he. "Oh, yes, you have thought of it very seriously. People always think seriously of the suggestions which poor old Caporno makes to them. Very! Yes, you have thought of it! What have you decided?"

It angered me a little, but not as much as you would suspect. I was more and more entertained. I felt that this rascal was no more to be trusted than a wildcat, or a thunderbolt! Yet I was immensely charmed by him and his very violence, his insolence, his conceit, his enormous egotism which seemed to embrace the entire world.

Pedro had poured the wine.

Caporno raised his glass and squinted at the fountain through it.

"As for the idea which –" I began.

"Be quiet one instant. I am about to drink!" said Caporno.

Thus he drank. First he took a sip. Then he took a small swallow. Then he smacked his lips loudly and shook his head from side to side, grimacing with ecstasy. Only then did he finish off the glass.

He lay back with a sigh of weariness and extended the glass, which Pedro received.

"Ah," said Caporno, "wine is delicious, but an effort. Gin, tequila, brandy, whisky – they are a small effort to drink. One need not use one's heart. One need not pour out one's soul into the glass. But with wine – it is very hard to make myself, every time I raise the glass, say: 'This is the first time I have tasted it. What is this strange liquid?' Very hard, and harder still to cheat my nose and make it believe that it has never inhaled that same identical fragrance before. Well, you were saying what? Something of no importance – folderol to the effect that you saw no reason why you should come to live with me in my house! Am I right?"

"You are right," said I. "Except that it is not folderol, as you call it."

"Ah, young men, young men, what fools they are!" sighed Caporno. "How they waste the precious hours and the opportunities of life – thinking, judging, hesitating, making choices. Do you not know, Mendez, that the one thing of importance is to live?"

"Señor," said I, "I learn from you!"

He twisted his head violently toward me.

"Yes," said he, "I think that you may have enough sense to learn!"

CHAPTER 12

After this, his manner changed suddenly.

"Now, my young friend," said he, "let us talk frankly and seriously to one another; in the first place, you are right in not drinking with me. In the second place, time flies and we must get on with our business, must we not?"

"As you please, señor," said I, and I glanced sharply at Pedro.

The old man paid no heed to me, but Caporno, though he had not seemed to take the slightest notice of me, was instantly aware of the meaning of that look of mine.

"As for Pedro," he said, "don't fear to speak out before him. He is a shadow, not a man. He is a spirit, not flesh. How close can you guess your own age, Pedro?"

"Since my eightieth year, I have been like a vain girl, Señor Caporno. I have not kept track of the birthdays."

"You do not look that age," I could not help saying – although, in fact, after inspecting him closely, he looked as old as a sheet of papyrus.

"That is a foolish compliment," said Caporno. "But there is no harm done. He cannot hear you."

"Señor? When he hears you so perfectly?"

"His ear is tuned to my voice. That is all. He has spent the last fifty years listening to me and studying me. Have you not, Pedro?"

"I have watched you, señor."

"You see that he will never agree with me. Because he is afraid of spoiling me. Me! However, pay no more attention to him. I keep him as a sort of skeleton at the feast. What I say to you he will hear. What you say to me is a closed book to him. Are you content?"

"As you will, then," said I.

"Very good. Speak first about yourself, because of course you know enough about me."

"I have heard something of you, señor."

"No, no, no!" said he, with a childish expression of annoyance. "You have heard a great deal. Every one talks about me. It is my pleasure to be talked about. I need much talk. Many words are a purgative that carry away the evil reputation. If it is only to damn me, I am glad to have people talk about me. Because too much damning turns the mind around on itself. My enemies protest too much about the evil that is in me, as though I were a devil. The world sees that I am not a devil. Suddenly it leaps to another extreme. It says that I am good. As I said before, you need not lie about it. You have heard how I cheated my people?"

"I have heard it," I admitted.

He nodded and rubbed his hands together.

"When there is too much blood in a man it needs letting. In the same way, I let the blood of my nation. I cooled them. I forced them to change the old constitution and draw up a new one, which is good. Had it not been for me, they would still be robbed to this day. They should write me down as their greatest bene-factor – their most perfect patriot. However, time will give me my reward!"

I could not help chuckling.

"In the meantime, you do not trust me," said he.

I was silent.

"Confess!" he insisted.

"Perhaps not, then," said I.

"Excellent! Then you sit down with opened eyes! However, you will find so much good in me that you will be astonished! Now that you know enough about me, tell me about yourself."

"What shall I tell you?"

"Whatever you please; as much as you please; no man can tell me too much about himself."

I decided to dose him with some of his own medicine.

"I believe," said I, "that knowledge concerning a man is a bitter medicine which is to be got by a prescription from a doctor."

"What prescription," said he, "had you for the knowledge which you admit that you have of me?"

"Ah," said I, "you are yourself the physician and apparently are not afraid to prescribe for your own health. As for myself, however, I am willing to tell you the story of my life. It is for your ear only, however, as I hate publicity."

"Agreed," said he, and he dropped his head upon his hand and looked down upon the ground, as one who did not wish to disconcert me with any close observation. I was all the more amazed by this behavior because of the abruptness and the terseness of his manner in preceding moments of our interview.

But as time went on, I saw that this was not delicacy on his part. It was rather a desire to center his whole mind more forcibly upon what I had to say to him, and therefore, he would not waste any force by fixing his eyes upon me. I could feel, from moment to moment, the keenest criticism of what I had to say.

It was as blunt and as matter of fact as I could make it.

I said: "The family of Mendez comes from northern Spain."

"I think that it has a Castilian ring," said Caporno politely.

"On the contrary," said I, "we come from Arragon."

"By that I am not so well pleased," said he.

"In the course of our family history," said I, "we have never distinguished ourselves in the arts of peace."

He cast one side glance at my blunt, ugly features, made for sustaining blows, and at my thick, wide shoulders, made for dealing them.

"I believe it," said he.

"Except for one bishop," said I, "and he was disgraced and read out of orders because, in the midst of a campaign, he, too, violently sacked and burned a town."

Caporno made a faint clucking sound, and I knew that the rascal's sympathy was not for the ruined inhabitants of that fictitious town.

"But, aside from this one peaceable flaw," said I, "we have been distinguished rather as people who knew various ways of breaking the law, almost all by violence. My ancestors were famous for their intimate knowledge of the landscape. They knew every narrow ravine and every dark passage of the mountains of Arragon. They knew every fellow who could be corrupted by a gold piece and turned into an assistant villain. Accordingly, they carried on their depredations so very luckily that they were never arrested without having enough money hidden away in their mountain holds to corrupt the judgment of the king or of the king's ministers."

Here Caporno saw fit to interrupt my tale by straightening in his chair and breaking into the heartiest but the most silent laughter – so immoderate that it lasted for some moments and in the end he had to wipe the tears from his eyes.

"This is delightful!" said he. "They remained rough brigands in the mountains to the end, then?"

"Not at all," said I. "We were always careful to maintain one member of the family – some bold, adroit, and cunning man of a pleasing address, near the person of the king himself. This representative of the family was always notable for his generosity to the clergy, his charity to the poor, his amiable conversation, his prudent relief of his fellow nobles –"

"Nobles?" said Caporno, darting in the question like the flicker of a sword blade across the conversation.

"Ah, señor," said I a little sadly, "ingenuous though I am trying to be with you, you surely will not ask me to give you my full title?"

"Have you not mine?" said he testily.

"And what is your title?" I asked, assuming a passion of sudden scorn which was uncontrollable. "What is your title – except that of chief legal thief?"

He did not explode with passion. He merely said: "Whereas you, my dear friend?"

"Whereas my people," said I, "have robbed under the very hand of one of the greatest kings in Christendom and singed the beards of the generals who were sent out to drag them into the courts of justice."

"This is beautiful," said Caporno with an astonishing humility. "I accept the rebuke. Pray continue."

"As I have said, we maintained one representative in the court of the kings, and this man was usually of the greatest value to us when we fell into times of trouble, for he would know exactly what hands must be crossed with silver and what hands must be crossed with gold, before our arrested and suspected men could regain their freedom. You will understand how this could be?"

"Most perfectly," answered Caporno, smiling.

"In this manner," said I, "we have gone on down the ages, robbing gayly, sometimes not with impunity, and yet again with great success, distinguished in the wars to which our country has been a party, distinguished also for our piety."

"Ha?" cried Caporno.

"Piety," said I.

"But how could that be?"

"With part of the spoils which my ancestors have taken in war – and in peace – they have built a great church which stands across a mountain valley and its golden chimes makes music through –"

"That is enough," interrupted Caporno with a slight touch of disgust, I thought. "You need not grow poetical about the virtues of your ancestors."

"At least," I could not help adding, "there was never a Mendez – who ever formed part of the procession at an auto-da-fé. No, our religion was perfect. Our politics were perfect, also. It was only in the very little matter of the legality of certain small actions –"

"I understand."

"At length, however, we fell upon evil days. My grandfather turned out a law lover. He was a lawyer and a famous one. He interrupted our grand succession of knaves. He broke off our intercourse with ruffians and assassins. He left to my father a perfect desire to resume the grand old family ways, but a perfect inability to keep at the work. All the means, as you will see, had been stripped from his hands. He attempted to remake the old trails, but he slipped upon them and spent the greater part of his life in prison. I, his son, recognized that there was a limited opportunity in the Old World, and therefore I was determined to try the manners and methods of the new one. And here you find me!"

CHAPTER 13

Here I paused, and the other began to nod and frown to himself and drum the tips of his fat fingers together. At last, he began humming, but still he did not look at me.

"Enchanting," said he. "Most enchanting, dear Mendez. So you are only newly come to our little New World?"

"I have been here these many years."

"With good fortune?"

Perhaps it was a foolish thing to do. But I certainly did not do it for ridiculous vanity. It was merely because, in studying this fat fellow before me, I felt that he was bound to be very deeply mixed in the next events of my life, and I thought that this might be the proper manner in which to impose upon him. At any rate, I took out my wallet and tossed it to him.

I expected, of course, that he would simply give one glance to the contents. But that was not Caporno! He took out every item of money in the wallet – I thanked heaven that there was nothing but money in it! – and counted the paper slowly, with great leisure, with apparent delight, smiling and nodding to himself all of the time. He stacked the hundred-dollar bills by themselves and the twenties in other stacks, and so with the tens and fives.

"Twenty-seven hundred and fifty dollars!" said he at last. "That is not much in a way, and yet it is a great deal in another way. How old are you, my dear son?"

I hesitated for the briefest instant. It was true that I looked thirty or a bit more – at least, according to my own opinion. It was also true that my opinion might not be that of Caporno. There was a mortal shrewdness in the bright eyes of that fat rascal which frightened me and told me that it would be well to proceed most cautiously with him.

I decided, ultimately, that I would split the difference between the truth and what I felt to be the appearance.

"I am twenty-five," said I.

Here he did at last swing around upon me, with a soft chuckling distorting his face.

"Twenty-five?" said he. "My dear Mendez – my dear, foolish, delightful boy!"

I hardly knew whether or not he was

laughing at me because he thought that I was overstating or understating my age. At last I decided, almost savagely, that on this one point I should allow him to know the truth.

"As a matter of fact," said I, "it is sometimes necessary for a man to make a pretense."

"So long as it is not ridiculous," he answered me instantly.

"Then I shall tell you the whole truth. I am twenty-two, señor!"

But here he stiffened in his chair and smashed his hands violently together.

"Ten thousand devils!" cried he. "Twenty-two? You? This is worse and worse! Pedro!"

The aged skeleton stepped in before me.

"Look at that man as if he were a horse and tell me what his age may be! Forgive me if I doubt you, Mendez! We must know the truth early in our acquaintance!"

The old Pedro gave me what I thought was only a passing glance, and then he said to his master: "This gentleman is a little above twenty – beneath his beard, señor!"

Then he stepped back into his corner.

Señor Caporno clapped his hands loudly together. He seemed delighted, and I think that he was, although his delight was based upon his own mistake.

"Ah, amigo!" cried he. "What a fool I was

making of myself, for I should have called you thirty years old to a day – yes, or more! My dear Mendez – my dear son – my dear child – do you forgive me for my doubt?"

I could not help smiling on him. From what I have reported of his conversation you may think that this good nature of mine was rather strange, but as a matter of fact, there was a charm in this rascal which I cannot report or sum up accurately in words. There was a fragrance, I may say, which surrounded him, and which was born of nothing.

"I forgive you, of course," said I.

"Then our bargain is concluded," said he.

"I do not exactly know to what you refer," said I.

"That is nonsense!" He frowned upon me as he said it. "Of course you are perfectly aware that what I mean is that I desire to employ you and pay you regular wages for your services!"

I smiled on him again, but I said nothing. I felt, in a way, that I knew how to handle this man. So I continued to smile, and smiling, I rose from my seat, and still smiling I bowed in farewell to him.

"*Peste!*" snapped he. "I should have called it a salary, if you are intending to be punctilious."

I said: "My dear Señor Caporno, I cannot tell

116

what section of your native land produced you, but I assure you that in Arragon, we are afflicted with what you might call national idiosyncrasies – "

"Confoundedly proud, I suppose!" he said, smiling at me. "I hate pride," he added.

I bowed to him again. "I shall trouble you no longer," said I. "I have enjoyed the chat and the pleasant drink, señor."

I was backing away from him.

"Pedro!" gasped Caporno, and his face swelled and turned purple until I actually thought that blood vessels must instantly burst. "Pedro! In the name of heaven, stop him!"

The ancient Pedro glided instantly beside me, and laid upon my arm a withered hand which was rather appealing than restraining. I could not shake off the grasp of that mummied hand. In fact, I did not wish to do so, and I was only waiting for a favorable opportunity to accept the invitation of Caporno to remain and listen to him. Yet I had felt, and I still felt, that if I allowed him to take me too casually, I would mean to him no more than a dog, and that was an attitude which I was determined to prevent.

"You devil, Mendez," stammered and gasped Caporno. "Ah, Lord, there is the gout again. You have ruined my day. May you be damned because you know that you are necessary to me! Sit down. No, if you are proud – I beg you on my knees to sit and listen to me!"

Of course I sat down at once and told him I was sorry if I had disturbed him very much. He lay back in his chair for a time, mopping his forehead and sighing, and taking his breath again noisily, and all the time, flashing side glances at me as though he wished to make sure that I was still there and had not sneaked away from him.

"Ah, Mendez, that was cruel!"

"I did not intend it so!"

"All young men are brutal!"

"Forgive me, señor."

"I meant salary, Mendez, not wages! On my honor, that was my meaning!"

"You are kind."

"Lad, you are still cold to me. Why?"

"Señor, the family of Mendez –" I began.

He broke in: "Is not accustomed to taking service. Is not that what you would say?"

"You have put it very tersely."

"You would not serve. You would be acting as a savior to my family."

"In what way, may I beg of you?"

"*Peste!*" cried he, bringing out that most unSpanish oath with a rich flavor. "I must explain everything! Yet my habit is to buy a man first and then afterward explain – ten thousand pardons, Mendez! I did not mean to hint that I was buying –"

"I am not offended!"

"Curse your pride!" breathed he. "It has me upon pins and needles every moment!"

"I am sorry."

"The salary, first."

"I had rather learn the nature of the employment, señor."

"Your employment is to condescend to be a protector to my family!"

"Señor, you are pleased to be merry!"

"I? I am the soul of gravity! I swear! I beg of you to consider yourself in the position of a member of the family!"

"You are too kind, indeed!"

"As for the salary –"

He paused and stabbed me with another flashing side glance like the sliding of a keen knife.

"The salary is five thousand dollars a year!" he cried.

It bewildered me a little – plainly. For four years, living as I had lived upon the spoils of the spoilers, striking where I chose to strike, collecting rich booty three or four times a year and gathering in more thousands than I could ever hope to spend with ease, money had meant little or nothing to me.

A thousand a year was sufficient for my needs – enough to keep me in food and ammunition, buy an occasional new gun, and fill the palm of my friends in the mountains – the fellows who, here and there, I could count upon for information and harborage, in time of need. Such had been my life. But, in the days preceding, a man who had five thousand dollars for an income could hardly be a laborer. Even the head boss of a big ranch would not get, perhaps, more than a hundred a month. So, the thought of the five thousand staggered me a little.

I hope that I did not show emotion, however. When one has had to look danger gravely in the face as often as I had had to look at it before my twentieth year, one gains, at the least, a fair control of one's outward expression. Yet, under the steel-pointed eyes of Caporno, how could I tell what I had revealed?

"Five thousand a year is a handsome thing," I admitted.

"I see that you like it," said he. "But what will you think, when I tell you, my dear boy, that five thousand a year is only a small beginning with me? In fact, it is only introductory to my real hopes of what I may be able to do for you! The possibilities are almost limitless!

Mendez, if I can find a man whom I can trust, I tell you that millions and millions may pass through his fingers — and where millions pass through the fingers, is it not impossible that a few of the dollars should not stick to the skin which handles them?"

He said it with an air of the greatest significance.

"Señor," I broke in rather abruptly, "you are making great professions. You have known me for less than half an hour!"

"False! I have known you for a thousand years. For the instinct in me is a thousand years old, at least; and that instinct learns when it stands face to face with an honest man!"

"Señor, you overwhelm me!"

"Then you are with us? You accept a place in my family, my boy?"

"Señor, you are kind. I am as far from your service as ever until I learn — what that service may be."

"Come, come!" said he darkly. "There are limits! Do not try to impose upon me too far!"

"I am adamant!" said I. "A Mendez must know everything before he can take employment."

I thought of my rough, old past, and could have smiled at myself.

"Very well," said he, dark with gloom. "I

shall tell you briefly, because, hearing, I know that you will not be afraid. Señor, I tell you that at this moment my happiness stands in danger of the most dreadful and the most famous single warrior in the whole range of the mountains."

"I am sorry to hear it," said I. "What is his name?"

"His name is one that you must be familiar with, no matter how short a time you have been in this district. His name, my friend, is Hugo Ames, and from the danger of his hand I expect you to protect me and mine!"

CHAPTER 14

Of course I was surprised. I showed it.

"You have heard?" he asked anxiously. "Are you afraid to undertake such a task?"

"I have heard of him as a ruffian," said I. "I confess that I am not afraid of any dishonest man!"

"That is a very stupid speech, but a very brave one," decided Caporno.

"How can such a desperado – living hundreds of miles from this house – how can he have become your deadly enemy, señor?"

"He is not my enemy. He is the enemy of one in my house! It is for the particular protection of that person that I enlist you. But do you accept my proposal?"

"Señor," said I, after a moment in which I had turned the proposal backward and forward in my mind, "I accept for some limited time."

"Six months is as good as forever. Your pay

shall be advanced to you. Mendez, I am enchanted! Pedro, he is mine. Ah, this is truly a happy day!"

Rising from his chair, he seized on me with one hand and upon Pedro with the other. At the same instant, it seemed to me that his exultation made the pangs of his gout to disappear – his unwieldy bulk was borne upon his feet as lightly as the slender body of any youth. The grip of his hand had in it a force which astounded me. In his own youth, surely, Señor Caporno was a man of might.

He was still laughing and clapping his hands together, congratulating himself, when he lowered himself into his chair again. He called for wine and the next ten minutes was devoted to cursing Pedro as that old worthy offered two different glasses, neither of which was of correct temperature. At last, the right degree was found, and the old voluptuary sat back in his chair and sipped the wine until the glass was empty.

"Ah," said he when that was done, "there is nothing like the reward of an excellent draft at the end of a day of good work! All of my day's work is boiled down into this interview with you, my dear young friend!"

"Will you answer some questions?"

"I hate questions, but you are too new a

friend to be refused. Continue!"

"Who is the person I am to protect?"

"You have seen him riding, I have no doubt, at the side of my beautiful daughter – he whom I mean is Mr. Lewis Vidett."

"He is not Spanish!" I exclaimed.

"As charming as though he were, however. Quite!"

"It is Mr. Vidett I am to care for?"

"Not he alone, but my daughter also!"

"What!" said I, "is this Ames such a devil that he would cut the throat of a woman, also?"

"Ames! I have named only the smaller half of the danger to you! Only the smaller half!"

It gave me, of course, a severe shock. There was something infinitely soothing in the thought that the only danger from which I was to guard this old rascal was Ames, or, in a word, the true self of which Francisco Mendez was the ghost. But now it appeared that there were still other troubles to be faced in the future.

"There is another danger greater than that from Ames?" I asked. "In the first place, why is Ames an enemy? How in the name of the devil can you have come to offend this outlaw?"

"I?" said Caporno, making a large gesture. "My son, my hand has stretched across the world, and has been felt by people of all nations. There is not a country in the world where you will not find men who want my heart's blood!"

He said this nodding to himself and chuckling and leaning back in his chair rubbing his hands. I think that I have never seen even a painted face with half so much evil in it as there was in the face of Caporno at that moment. Yet it was rather like a boy who revels in the mischief which he has made.

"In the meantime," said he briskly, "we have gripped hands and made the bargain, have we not?"

"I shall sign a paper, also," said I, "if you wish me to do so."

"Signatures are a waste of time," said he. "The record of my life in ink would not fill half a page in a copy book, but that same record in the hearts of men – and women also – would fill a library of fat volumes. But now you must meet Lewis Vidett. Pedro!"

Pedro apparently had followed the last speech of his master. He himself did not go to execute the order, but he lifted a hand and from behind him an agile, soft-footed servant glided out and stood beside the old man. The command of Pedro was repeated in a murmur which I could not overhear; and the servant instantly vanished.

Caporno went on: "Vidett is a gallant boy, Mendez. To see him is to love him, as my daughter found. You will imagine that I would not give her readily to a nameless young adventurer like Vidett. But what could I do? What could I do? Shall I tell you the story of how he came wooing her?"

I admitted that I was very curious. He began at once, hurrying a little because he could not tell at what moment Vidett himself would appear upon the scene.

"I was at that time the president of a flourishing young republic – not so flourishing as it became afterward, however, when I had taught it certain lessons in economy, you may be sure. However, all was well. My policies were popular. The poor believed that I was an honest rich man and the rich believed that I was a clever rich man. So that all classes were satisfied – and all classes were deceived! It was at about this time in my career that I gave a great ball and at the ball my daughter appeared – my lovely girl – my beautiful Rosa! However, you have seen her, and I shall not waste words even upon such a subject.

"She was the star of the evening. She dazzled old and young and even gray-faced elders smiled and grew foolish in the eye when they passed near her. As for Rosa, she passed like an enchantress among the creations of her own mind – quite untouched among the havoc which she was making with her smiles and her laughter. When she danced, all eyes trailed about the great room after her.

"I was, of course, pleased. Every father is delighted when he sees his daughter making a fool of other men. It is a reward. It is a revenge, you may say, for the hours in one's own youth when one has been tangled in the net of some silly girl and danced attendance on her, lost in a crowd. Even I, even Caporno, have been in that position! Will you believe it?"

I could not help laughing at this childish vanity. But he was not offended.

"Laugh if you please," said the old villain. "Laugh with me or laugh at me. Only silent men I fear! To continue, I was delighted when I saw my daughter scattering destruction and leaving broken hearts on either side of her as thick as the seeds which the sower scatters. Very well, thought I. Play your game. Enjoy your pleasures. May they last long before you are caught – or before it is necessary for me to tell you!"

"What?" exclaimed I.

"Are you shocked?" said that scoundrel of a Caporno. "But of course, one of the chief reasons for my pleasure in her beauty was that

I hope some day to take advantage of it for a good match. But let me get on. Yet I begin to fear that you are a distressingly moral young man. Morality is a leaden anchor. One cannot climb far or high with such a weight.

"I continue: Toward the end of the ball, instead of a silken rustle of applause, a little wave of silence and sharp attention followed my Rosa. When I looked, I saw the reason. The other young men and the middle-aged widowers – they had fallen away from her. Only one knight remained to escort her. He was very young – handsome as a god – light-footed – light-handed – with a smile to stop the heart of a girl and very gay blue eyes.

"As beautiful as a woman, and yet, all manly! Do you understand? There was not a thing feminine or weak about him. He was graceful – but there was strength behind his grace. He was gentle and gay, but it was the gentleness and the gayety of a fearless heart!

"I looked, and I saw the danger. But I did not dream how far the fever had spread even by this time. I did not dream! But that night, after we had returned to the house, I came to understand!"

CHAPTER 15

At this point, Caporno paused and glanced to the side, and I saw walking toward me that same slender and sprightly youngster whom I had watched before, as he rode at the side of the girl with the four horsemen in attendance behind them. This, then, was Lewis Vidett. This was the man whom I was to guard.

However, I could not, first of all, help agreeing that he was all man. One, surely, would never have dreamed that such a man as this was in any need of a guard. His step, as Caporno had told me, was light, and his smile was as smooth and as bright as the smile of any girl. Yet there was the elasticity of strength about him. He carried his head in that nameless way – high and yet easily – which denotes a man of heart.

I respected him the instant I laid eyes upon him. He was at the best not more than a fellow of average weight and height; and I had my bulk of two hundred and twenty pounds of hard bone and athletic muscle to pit against him; yet I tell you frankly that I should not have entered upon a quarrel with that fellow freely. I would have avoided him as I would have avoided a wildcat.

He came with his light step and his smile under the barred shadows of the colonnade toward Caporno, and I saw the heavy, sinister face of that swarthy gentleman light with a flash of pleasure.

That instant, I knew that he loved his son-in-law to be. Yet he raised his hand and waved.

"I am not ready for you yet, Lewis. Amuse yourself, my child, for another moment. Then I shall be ready for you."

Vidett answered with a graceful little gesture and turned out into the patio where he sat down on the rim of the fountain bowl and amused himself watching the blue jay, which was hovering heavily near by, eager to return to its perch beside the bright waters and almost un-afraid of the man. It was a pleasant sight to watch Vidett. As he sat there hugging his knees and laughing at the dancing bird in the air above him, I could not help smiling with pleasure.

"Yet," broke in Caporno suddenly, "he is

three years your elder! He is twenty-five. But what are years? It is the fountain of exhaustless youth which matters, and that bubbles in him constantly and gayly! Ah, divine gift!"

He sighed.

"However," he went on, "I come back to the evening after the ball when I sat discussing men and women with my wife. That was her one talent – or curse – the ability to gossip; personalities tumbled forever off her tongue. Well, as we sat talking, our Rosa came in to us. She paid no more attention to her mother than if she had been a statue of salt.

"There is a sense in that girl, and she knew that I was the one who mattered in the family.

"Up to me she stepped: 'I have found the man that I shall marry!' said she.

"Her mother screamed. 'That penniless young American fool!'

" 'Will you send my mother away?' said Rosa, not even looking at her.

" 'Impertinence!' screams Mrs. Caporno.

"But I understood. Not impatience – but brains! I send my wife away. I take her beneath the elbows and shove her, wriggling, from the room. Then I return to my girl.

" 'Is it madness, dear Rosa?' said I.

" 'Yes,' says she. 'It is madness.'

" 'Nevertheless, you shall not be married to an adventurer!'

" 'I will leave the house and go to him this instant!' says she.

" 'I shall have the puppy stabbed!'

" 'You shall not dare!' says she.

"By the heavens, when I look into her black eyes, I see that she is right.

" 'You love him?'

" 'I have said before – it is madness. I must have him!'

" 'What is he?' I ask her.

" 'You will see him for yourself,' says she.

" 'At least,' says I, 'he seems harmless.'

"She shrugs her shoulders.

" 'When can the marriage take place?' says she.

" 'In a month,' says I.

" 'It is too long!'

" 'In three weeks!'

" 'It is too long!'

" 'Rosa, you may marry him in two weeks from this night!'

"She threw herself on my neck and kissed me and told me that I was the kindest father in the world – and the wisest!

"However, before the two weeks ended, the revolution came. We traveled suddenly and unexpectedly across the sea and north to our new home. Even Rosa saw that it was best to have the house completed and all the family affairs settled before she married him. That is the reason why she is not wearing a golden ring at this moment. Do you understand them?"

"I think," said I, "that you have told me more than a little about both of them!"

He grinned at me, his fat face folding into old creases. "Very well, my son," said he, and he called briskly to Vidett.

The latter came at once. I stood up, and I felt his calm, bright glance ripple from my head to my feet, missing not a feature of my bulk. I felt that I was weighed. I felt, under that cold, bright blue eye, a little ashamed of my assumed Mexican finery. We were introduced. A slender hand touched mine.

What happened was my fault. God has given me more physical strength than any man needs, and above all, he has given me more strength in the hands. My grip is heavier than I know. After all, in my lonely life there had been few necessities of shaking hands. The pressure which I put upon his slender hand brought a flash into his eyes. The feminine brightness left them and was replaced by the glimmer of steel. His fingers coiled like taut springs. It was astonishing!

No, not that I could not have ground that

hand of his to a broken, helpless useless mass, but that I was astonished and delighted to see what power could leap out of a wrist so small. I said to him instantly: "I ask your pardon, señor. I did not mean to match strength with you!"

At that, he relaxed his hold and our hands parted; but I saw a swift, brief shadow of contempt fly across his face. It was very plain that he had misjudged me.

"Now, Lewis," said Caporno, "your troubles are ended; you can close your eyes at night without worry for Señor Mendez will not leave you day or night. He has become our guard. Best of all, he is your guard, Lewis. Señor Mendez is our surety against gunmen and knife fighters! Are you not, Mendez?"

I muttered that of course it was my duty to do my best. But I was not paying much attention to Caporno himself. I was too interested in this Lewis Vidett, this young American whom I had pledged myself to guard for six months' term, at least, and at a salary which seemed to me princely.

Of course there was a great deal for me to think of; but, first of all, I could not help wondering why I, now safely guarded from their recognition by beard, mustache, name and clothes, should be suspected as an enemy of a man whom I had never in my life seen before?

There was only one possible answer, it appeared. In the party of the four riders who had gone north to destroy poor Truck Janvers, this Lewis Vidett had been one. Ay, there was still another possibility. Perhaps it was through him that the four riders had started on their mission of blood!

Yet, when I concluded that there must be some connection between this brilliant young Vidett and that large-handed, slow-witted miner in the north country, I was amazed. However, it was for me to find it. I began to feel that I was standing in the presence of the man who was the cause of the death of Truck Janvers.

I cannot tell you how perfectly it hardened my heart! I turned as grim as a piece of steel. I was ready to look past all of the youth and the charms of this youngster and regard the facts which might lie beneath.

That he regarded me with not much greater favor was plain, for I felt his calm, cold eyes flicker over me as he said to Caporno: "Señor, I only ask: Why must I be guarded?"

"Why? Why? Why?" screamed Caporno. "Knife thrusts in the dark – gun shots from behind the trees – name of the heaven, child, do you ask me that seriously?"

"Ah, señor," said the boy, still eyeing me with a faint, discourteous smile of scorn which Caporno could not see, of course, from his chair, "but why should our new kind friend, Señor Mendez, be employed – at such an expense?"

There was a subtle insult conveyed in the last phrase that made me clench my teeth and Caporno heard the tone as well as I. He rasped out harshly: "Hear me, Lewis! I am in earnest. Now walk away with Mendez and come to an agreement, the two of you. Each of you will find that the other is a man! Now go!"

I went, accordingly, half unwillingly, at the side of the young Vidett. Why do I call him young, when he was three years my senior? Well, it was because, as Caporno himself had pointed out, the very spirit of youth was incarnate in Vidett. He guided me out of the patio, and we were instantly among the shadows of the trees. Then, whirling toward me with a smile, I saw the flash of a gun in his hand and before I could stir, he had fired!

Fear shot a hot bolt through me, like the tearing chunk of lead from the muzzle of his Colt which he had conjured out of nowhere. Yet, though the turn of Vidett had been fast as a flash of light, and though he had seemed to be looking me fairly in the eyes, he had found a target for his bullet.

Through the higher branches of a tree just behind me there began a light crashing, rapidly increasing in velocity and in volume until I looked over my shoulder just in time to see the little body of a tree squirrel, half-floated by its brushy tail, thud lightly and softly upon the ground.

CHAPTER 16

It was a masterful display of marksmanship. The draw, the swift spin of young Vidett's body, and the instant selection of a target were matters which I could appreciate – professionally, you might say. There is nothing like familiarity to breed contempt, says the old maxim, but I will aver that there is nothing like familiarity with the tricks, the whims, the uncertainties of a revolver to breed respect for the man who can use it with any degree of accuracy.

I have heard much talk of wonderful revolver play. But I have not seen a great deal of it. Most men, even at the shortest range, would do much better to depend upon the slowness and the accuracy of a rifle; the snap draw generally leads to a snapshot which hurts nothing but the wall of the room, or the empty air. But to gain any degree of skill with that weapon needs constant, constant practice, together with a certain amount of finger genius – I know of no other term which will express the thought.

I have always had a fair degree of natural talent with guns, but I never had the real genius. But what little talent I had, was carefully cultivated up to my eighteenth year. From that moment forward, during four years I had gone from day to day with the very sure knowledge that at any moment my life might depend upon my ability to get a gun out of leather fast and put my bullet fairly into the target. So I had worked patiently and steadily, of course. Not with a thrill of joy at my skill as I gradually acquired it, but with a sort of laborious earnestness and a grim fixation of purpose.

Often I was in such a place that I dared not risk the noise which guns make. In those cases, I had to fall back upon the mere handling of the weapon itself. People speak of the balance of a revolver, but at the best it is a clumsy weapon to manage until one has worked with it so long that it becomes simply an added part of the flesh.

When one can take his Colt to pieces in the dark and assemble it again – and all with as much speed as if the light were shining to show him what to do; and when one can jerk out his gun from its holster at the first alarm, finding it instinctively with his hand, as the call of a bird wakens him in his camp in the morning, or as the voice of a wild beast disturbs him at night – when a man has gone through a training severe enough to leave these effects in him, then he begins to be ready for real practice with lead at a target. Day by day, month by month, year after year, I labored and labored at that necessary craft. My revolvers did not last long. They were simply burned out by constant use, one after another, for the instant the gun ceased to shoot exactly true, it had to be discarded.

I say, therefore, that I was at least qualified to appreciate the wonderful adroitness of Vidett as he whirled and shot the squirrel out of the treetop. But by a great effort of the will I kept the slightest degree of that admiration and that shock from appearing in my eyes.

He was saying, smiling in his insulting, superior way: "Now we are out of earshot of that old fool, and we can speak our minds. Tell me, my most respected Señor Mendez, why I need you or any other man as a bodyguard?"

"I do not wish to pose as a teacher," said I.

"You are modest," said he, and still his insolent gaze was swinging up and down my body, as though he were finding a thousand vulnerable places in me – things to be mocked – bits of my new-bought finery which were out of keeping with the character of a gentle-man.

"However," said I, "when I see a mistake, I have to try to alter it – seeing that a very young man is making the mistake!"

"I am afraid," said he coldly, "that that is a piece of impertinence."

"My dear Señor Vidett," said I, "do not consider that I have the slightest interest in what you say or in what you think or feel, but what I am interested in is the man who is employing me – with most liberal wages!"

Color leaped into his face and fire into his eye. He looked at me steadily. The steadiness of a puma as it stalks its prey. There was something inexpressibly deadly and formidable about that handsome youngster the instant he left off smiling and became serious. Perhaps he knew it, and that was the reason that a smile was almost never off his lips.

The sinister expression altered a little almost at once, however.

"You are a cool rascal," said he. "Señor Mendez, you are very cool. And very impertinent. But there is no reason why I should murder a man for impertinence – so long as a third ear does not hear him!"

"Thank you," said I sardonically. "You relieve me a great deal!"

"Impertinent still! However, what is there wrong in my marksmanship?"

"You refer to your lucky hit on the squirrel?" said I.

"Lucky?" said he, letting his cold smile return.

Of course it was skill – but there was luck in it – an immense portion of luck! I knew too much about marksmanship to think that any one who ever lived could have turned and made that hit in that fashion without having a very liberal portion of luck at his side.

"Luck," I repeated, "as you very well know. However, it is plain that you could have improved upon your work, for every one knows that a squirrel is useless game when a body hit is made and the creature is blown half to tatters – whereas there is a serviceable hide and good food remaining when the head is nipped off."

"That is absurd," said he. "But I should be very happy to see you demonstrate what you mean – by a snapshot like mine!"

I had invited that remark, of course. But I saw that my case was desperate. I had to demonstrate some skill of an extraordinary kind, or this youngster would begin by despising me, and under the burden of his contempt I could not, of course, live in that house with any content whatever. I was ready for the invitation. My fingers were already curling for the draw of my Colt. In my mind, I had been marking the exact spot at which I had seen the body of the squirrel strike the ground and how far I should have to turn in order to fire at it.

So, in answer to him, I said with a smile: "Of course I am very happy to oblige you. It should be done in this manner."

I flipped out the heavy Colt which was concealed under my right armpit and I fired with my left hand instantly, hardly stirring my body at all.

Luck was with me as luck had been with him. Frankly it was a thing which I could not expect to duplicate in more than one chance out of four. But this was my fortunate chance. The head was snipped fairly from the body of the poor little squirrel as it lay bleeding on the ground, and my smoking revolver was instantly back in its hiding place.

"Because," I went on, hardly changing my tone or interrupting myself by the bit of target shooting, "because, my young friend, bullets in the body often do not kill – at once. As a rule it is advisable to kill – at once! So – the head, señor – the head!"

He was impressed. More than that, he showed that he was disturbed in mind by what he had seen. I had this advantage over him — that at first sight I had decided that he was an extraordinary fellow from whom almost anything could be expected. Whereas he had seen in me simply a heavy-handed boor, celebrated for the moment in that valley of the San Marin because with a blow of my fist I had broken the side of a man.

Deftness of any kind was outside of his expectation of me. Moreover, he had planned on astonishing me by making the gay merrymaker appear for a flash as the deadly gun fighter. All in all, luck and foresight and guessing could not possibly have favored me more. The exquisite Lewis Vidett was staring at me now with wide, dull eyes.

"By Lord!" he broke out. "You are extraordinary!"

"Señor," said I, "you are too kind in saying this!"

He rubbed his knuckles across his chin and studied me above his hand.

"However," said he, "you will admit that it was largely a lucky shot which you made."

I smiled at him.

"As you please, señor," said I.

"Will you tell me," said he, frowning, "that you are actually in the habit of scoring in this fashion?"

"My dear friend," said I, "let us not ask too many questions of each other and we will get on much better together since I am to take charge of your safety."

"*You* are to take charge of it?" he asked in the most pointed fashion.

"It seems that I am."

"Have I not told you that I do not need assistance?"

"Ten thousand pardons! But I serve Señor Caporno, as you know."

"Is it possible that you would force yourself upon me?"

"Day and night – night and day," said I.

He uttered an exclamation of disgust and of wonder also.

"Does it not occur to you that this may be a dangerous service?"

"A profitable service, only."

"Mendez, do not be rash!"

"I am the height of caution!"

We stood for a moment regarding one another, he with a baleful stare and I with a forced smile. My smile managed to remain true only long enough. Then he stretched out his hand and laid it upon my arm.

"Mendez," said he, "I begin to think that we may become friends!"

"Vidett, I can wish for nothing more!"

146

"Shall we shake hands, then?"

Now, my own hand was half stretched out to him when a sudden thought stopped me. It was true that I was pledged to guard this man during six long months. It was also true that I suspected him of being either one of the murderers or a participant at least in the plans which brought about the destruction of poor Truck Janvers. My hands dropped back to my side.

"I prove my friends," said I, "before I take their hands."

A black scowl crossed the face of young Vidett.

"Very well!" said he. "If trouble comes out of this refusal of yours, remember that it is of your own choosing!"

CHAPTER 17

At this moment two servants, with weapons in their hands, came running toward us through the trees and, when they saw us, cried out. We learned from their first excited words that Señor Caporno, having heard the two shots in the trees, in an agony of alarm had sent out these messengers to find out what had happened to Vidett and to me.

Vidett and I, accordingly, went back with them and found Caporno sweating with excitement in the patio. He threw up his hands with a shout of joy when he saw us together.

"Do you know what I saw?" he cried to us. "I saw, at the first shot, the body of Lewis falling to the ground. Then, at the second shot, I saw Mendez leaning over him and, when the dying body stirred, sending a second bullet through his brain to end it all! Take my hands, both of you. Let me be sure that you have come back to me!"

Each of us took one of his fat hands, accordingly. Again I was amazed at the tremendous power in the fingers of that old luxury lover.

"You were testing one another in some diabolical way!" he cried, turning his head from one to the other.

"Perhaps," admitted Vidett carelessly.

"Oh, there is no devil like a young devil! You, Vidett, are also a great fool! Test this man, this Achilles, who breaks men with a touch of his hand? Test him?"

Vidett grew hot of face. "All strength is not in the hands," said he.

"Ah, there you speak like a young cutthroat. But, Lewis, in the name of heaven hear me and believe me! In many things you are too young to appreciate my wisdom. In many things, every old man seems an old fool to every youngster. But at least admit that I have the ability to read the print which concerns the hearts and the souls of men. In the face of this new friend of ours, our dear friend Francisco Mendez, I have seen a man slayer – a true destroyer! Will you believe it? Will you believe that it is suicide to raise your hand against him?"

He did not deliver this as a compliment, but he waved his hand toward me with a sort of horror, as one would point to a loathsome snake, ugly to behold, but irresistible because of the poison in its fangs. As for his protégé, he regarded me more calmly, but I felt that the words of his prospective father-in-law were of more than a little weight with him. I was glad of it. Frankly, I was afraid of that handsome youngster.

I was afraid of the lightning speed of his hand and the surety of his straight-looking eye. I felt that my safest way with Vidett was to maintain a sort of moral control over him, and nothing could have helped me in that direction more effectually than the words of Caporno.

"Now shake hands!" he commanded. "Let me see it done."

I gave my hand freely to Vidett, but with a reservation in my eye which he noted, I saw, at once.

"Go, now," said he to Vidett, "and send me Rosa. No, let Pedro go for her. I want her to see my new friend without a prejudice already in her eye!"

Vidett, accordingly, said good-by to me in the gayest manner and moved away, but I knew that there was more than one dark shadow of discontent in his mind. Pedro had disappeared into the house and now he came back behind the girl, came gliding back with a step as light as hers. Age seemed to wither and dry that man away, not really enfeeble him, no more than corpulent idleness had really affected the vigor of his ominous master. I could not help regarding the pair of them as a pair of devils. Which was the master devil?

Well, I was to learn that before the end!

But here was Rosa coming straight upon me. Here was I bowing before her, watching the dazzling flash of her teeth as she smiled at me. She stood beside the chair of her father looking down at him. I could not help noting that when she looked down in this fashion all the merriment and half the beauty seemed to disappear from her face and left there only a shade of sullenness and discontent.

Truly, from that moment I began to guess that there was something of her father in her; from that moment I was prepared to watch her closely. Well for me that I did!

Caporno was telling her as he had told Vidett that I had come into the house to be their guardian.

"Against what?" asked the girl, and lifted her black eyes toward me.

"Hush, my dear," said Caporno, with a secret frown at her. "In a word, I have not told him, except that he is to keep his eyes open."

"Ah?" said Rosa, and looked straight at me

again with her unfathomable eyes.

Yes, she was as exquisitely lovely close at hand as far away, but I preferred to look on her from the distance. Most of all, I felt that I would appreciate her in the highest degree if the lady had been locked in the frame of a picture and represented in dexterous paint alone! No, I did not like the daughter and the heir to Caporno's fortunes. The more I saw of her the more convinced I was that she would in the end get from him something more than his money alone.

These things were instincts, premonitions, but they glided across my brain with a very disagreeable strength for the moment.

"But you may tell him as much as you please," said Caporno, watching her thoughtfully.

"I don't understand, I hope," said the girl, staring steadily back at him in turn.

"You do, however."

"Everything?"

"Every syllable – if you think that it is wise!"

She shrugged her shoulders and turned back to me. "You have talked with Lewis Vidett, of course," said she.

"I have," said I.

"And Lewis," said her father with a world of dry meaning in his voice, "has come to an excellent understanding with my friend Mendez!"

At this, she started, and glanced askance at Caporno; and he met her eye with a nod.

"Ah?" said she again, with the same little lift in her voice which I had noticed before. This time, she looked on me with a great deal more respect.

"Will you come with me?" said Rosa, and took me to the farther end of the patio and let me sit down beside her in the shadow of the colonnade where we had an excellent view of Lewis Vidett as he strolled back and forth, seemingly wrapped up in delight in the flowers. For, now and again, he would pause and pick a new blossom and hold it up with a flourish.

"Do you see?" said the girl, staring at him. "Each time he throws away the old one!"

I did not understand her. As a matter of fact, I did not wish to understand her. Rosa's manner of thought was a bit too tipped with poison to be agreeable to me. I decided that I would not be too inquisitive in all of my dealings with her.

But she went on with an astonishing frankness – a frankness which was very disagreeable to me.

"I could not dare to talk with you except where he can see me," said she. "For, so long as he can see me, he does not care what I say. He is too able to read my mind in my face!"

She smiled upon me.

I thought that this was exceedingly odd conversation to a new acquaintance, however, and my attempt to answer that smile was a lamentable failure.

"You understand?" said she.

"Señorita," said I, "I haven't a very sharp mind. I really don't understand. Forgive me!"

Here I thought that she started a very little and looked more keenly aside at me. But I could not be sure.

Presently she said more gravely than ever: "I am glad of that. I think that I have never known as simple a man in my life!"

I was happy to say one honest word after all the half truths and the innuendoes among which I had been living for so much of this day.

"Señorita, in the name of heaven believe that I am no counterfeit!"

She laughed like the musical bubbling of water in a brook, far off. While she laughed, I remembered with a stab of conscience, how truly and vastly I was a counterfeit. For there was I in her father's house, hunting desperately for the slayer or the cause of the slaying of Truck Janvers, and with a grisly feeling in my heart that her lover, her handsome young

Lewis Vidett was the man that I wanted.

However, my answer on the face was honest enough. For I was a simple man and to this day I remain one! I leave dexterity of wits to those who prize such things!

"I do believe you," said she, when her laughter had died away pleasantly. "I do believe you! Now I am wondering if I cannot tell you, frankly, just what dangers you will be expected to face for us while you are in this house?"

"I hope that you may be open with me," said I.

She was studying me steadily, carefully, her eyes very busy with my features.

"I cannot tell!" said she at last. "It may be real honesty – and my father apparently thinks that it may be. But the danger is too terrible! Señor, I cannot confide in you – as yet. But perhaps the day will soon come!"

You will imagine that it was a little difficult to hear oneself analyzed and rejected as not quite the pure quill. I managed to keep my face fairly well in spite of those prying eyes, however.

"And," she went on, "seeing that I have to come to know you better, I suppose there isn't a bit of reason why I should keep you here just now – and keep my poor Lewis on pins and needles every second of the time you stay."

I stood up. She rose with me and gave me her hand. I almost liked the impulsive light in her eyes.

"I hope that we shall understand each other better when we sit together again!" said she.

"Señorita, it is my hope also!"

I left her in that fashion.

CHAPTER 18

When I sat in the room which had been assigned to me that night, I thought the matter over carefully. I mean, the whole affair and every one connected with it, and I assure you that there was not a single face in the entire group that appealed to me. Whether the young and handsome faces of Vidett and Rosa, or the old evil ones of Caporno and Pedro, or of José, whose villainly I had tested with a consummate accuracy, I knew not which I disliked most intensely. No, I cannot say that. For, from the very first moment, I loathed and hated Lewis Vidett with an absorbing passion of revolt.

Now, then, sitting in my room, I told myself that I was at last consigned to a nest of vipers and that any moment might be my last moment in life. A very grim situation, and yet there was something appealing about it, of course, as you can well imagine.

I undressed finally. I was in pajamas, blowing out the light, when a whisper from the window iced my blood.

"Hugo Ames!"

I did not hesitate. There were two windows leading to my room, and each was a big casement, and each was wide open. From one the hissing whisper had come. It was through the other that I leaped the next instant and landed on my bare feet on the soft flagstones beneath the colonnade of the patio.

I saw the man I wanted crouched beside the other casement, in the act of peering cautiously into it, and in his hand there was the deadly glimmer of steel. He did not see me; he could not; but I suppose that my hurtling flight through the other window must have made a noise like that of a gust of wind, and then there was the soft thudding of my feet and my hands on the flags.

It stiffened him with fear and surprise that kept him from whirling about for an instant, and that instant of delay was what I needed. I leaped again, and he was not halfway turned around when my weight ground him against the wall of the house. My shoulder bore against his chest and crunched the wind out of his lungs at a single pressure.

It was so thorough that I did not have to

pause to ask questions or to strike a blow. The fellow was as limp as a half-filled sack. So I simply chucked him through the window and heard him fall with a flop on the floor of my bedchamber. Then I bounded after and kindled the lamp which I had just blown out. Its light showed me a twisted form on the floor. I picked it up by the hair of the head and found myself looking down on the features of José!

My stomach grew as small and as hard as a clenched fist. How much had this rat talked in the house of his suspicions that I was the same man who had accompanied him from the north – a little distance in his rear? For, if he had spoken so much as a single word, I could be reasonably sure that Caporno would finish the guesswork and cut the Gordian knot with a swift touch of the knife!

I threw a glass of water in the face of José and sat down to watch him gasp back his breath. He was in an agony until he could breathe easily again, and, after that, he crouched in a corner against the wall, gaping at me. I have never seen fear so eloquent in any face.

"Tell me, José," said I gently.

He made an eloquent gesture with both of his hands.

"Kill me at once!" breathed he.

"Tell me," said I, "why did you not fire at

once through the window and then ask questions about me afterward?"

He drew in a gasping breath, as though he were still expecting death from my hand.

I added to explain to myself: "You were not quite sure, José? The beard fooled you? And the mustaches with the sharp points? So you had to ask the question first? Oh, foolish José!"

A spasm of terror and of regret flashed into his eyes, at that.

"I meant you no harm, señor," he vowed to me.

"No more harm, certainly, than you did when you stole the mule and went off on its back."

The rascal stared wildly around him. "Ah, señor," said he at last, "my heart was breaking with terror of you! With the rising of every sun I wondered in what form my death would come at your hands before it set again!"

I shook my head and still smiled at him. "You lie foolishly but completely, José," said I. "You lie very foolishly, because remember that I lived with you for whole weeks, and you understood that I could not injure a man who had drunk my liquor and eaten my food and accepted my care through all of that time – through all of that time when he might have been rotting on the side of the mountain – eh,

José? A white skeleton, by this time!"

"Ah, señor, how I have sinned against you!" cried out José, with so much frankness that my heart thrilled in me. "I also know," he went on, "that you will not harm me now, as I lie helpless in your hands, after you have given me so much kindness! You have poured it out upon me like water."

"On a desert – yes! No, José. I am allowing you to live for these few moments because I have not yet been able to decide in exactly what form I shall deal out a death to you. Death, of course, it must be. In self-respect – as a man with a duty to other men, I must, of course, kill you!"

José licked his dry lips. He tried to speak and brought forth only a dry whisper.

"I have thought of the whip, and a night of exposure to the sharp air. That is a slow death, when the back is flayed. Slow, certain, and terrible. But then there is much to be said in favor of a fire built of green wood so that the flames are always in a low welter. Those flames would rot off your feet in the fire. There would be time enough for you to make your prayers. Time enough for you to do everything except sing your hymns, because, of course, I should have to gag you first. Perhaps, the pain might make you strangle on the gag! That would be the most merciful thing, José."

"Señor!" breathed he. "Ah, in the name of a kind God!"

"In His name," said I coldly, "I cared for you after you had sneaked up on me to cut my throat as I slept. Who sent you on that errand, José?"

To my astonishment, even in his fear of death, he retained his fear of his master.

"Señor, I wish to tell you," whimpered José, who was fast breaking down.

"Consider. You speak life – or death for yourself! Answer me everything you have in your heart, and perhaps I shall let you live, my friend!"

He wriggled halfway across the floor toward me, writhing his body half like a snake. It was a frightful thing to watch the hope of life, like a new birth, flare across the mind of that villain.

"Will you swear that?"

"How will you have me swear?"

"Your hand – in my hand, señor! An honest man's oath!"

I put out my hand, and, reading my face desperately with his eyes, he clung to that hand with both of his. It was strangely prayerful!

Then he released me reluctantly. I showed him my good faith by deliberately putting up my gun, but he merely smiled at that.

"Ah, señor," said he, "do not play with me. I have seen you with more than the speed of a striking snake. Even Señor Vidett could only gaze and marvel at you!"

"You followed us through the trees?" said I.

"I did. I had your life in the crook of this finger." The rogue could not help grinning at the delightful thought.

"But?"

"But then Señor Vidett began to speak kindly to you. I could not tell – the hair had changed your face. I was not sure! And so – here I am!"

His gesture plainly called himself a fool.

"Who sent you to me tonight?"

He dragged himself half erect and approached my ear with his trembling, chalky lips.

"Señor Vidett!"

I had expected "Caporno" for an answer. It was a distinct shock.

"Vidett?" I said with as much assurance as I could summon. "And who sent you riding north to kill Truck Janvers?"

"Señor Vidett!"

Here, at last, was an answer for which I was more than half prepared, and yet being prepared did not ease the sense of shock entirely. For I still kept the picture of the death of poor Janvers before my eyes.

"Vidett sent you north?"

"Yes."

"Vidett knows that Hugo Ames followed you south, then?"

"Yes."

"Vidett knows that you suspect me of being Ames?"

"No."

I caught him by the throat with one hand and pressed him to his knees. He had barely room in his windpipe to gasp out: "I shall speak the truth!"

"Very well," said I, and relaxed my hold again.

"The truth is this, señor: I spoke to him and I told him that I suspected."

"And he?"

"He swore that no man in the world would dare to be so bold!"

"Ah?"

"I was to spy on you tonight and try some little test – he suggested this one of your name – and then to watch your face! I did not dream that it would bring you leaping out at a window behind me!" He shuddered.

"You will go back to Vidett?"

"At once!"

"And tell him?"

"That I was a fool to dream of such a thing!"

"José, if I trust you, I put my life in your hands!"

He stared at me for a moment as though he did not comprehend.

"Ah, señor," said he at the last, "have I not sworn to you the Americans' own oath?"

He smiled like a child who has struck upon a truth brighter than a shining diamond. I could not help but believe that he would be true to me, even after I tested him twice and found such villainy in his heart.

CHAPTER 19

José went to deliver a lying report to his master; I went back to my bed, and I slept soundly, because it is my good fortune to have such nerves, that in time of need they steady like steel and allow me to rest perfectly. To that fact alone I can attribute the hundred lucky escapes I have had from sure death.

I slept soundly, and I awakened in the morning to find myself an accepted member of the household. I was taken in among them most smoothly and without friction. We all met at the breakfast table. That is to say, every one was there with the exception of Señor Caporno himself, who lay on a couch at the side of the room where the sunshine would fall across his body. The ancient Pedro went softly back and forth waiting upon him, and the loud voice of Caporno filled the room.

I noticed in the very first place one

astonishing thing – that Rosa and Lewis Vidett listened to every word which the older man said, but that they paid not the slightest mental heed to him. Their faces were the masks of attention when he spoke, and I began to surmise that there were things in this household and its ways of which Señor Caporno did not guess.

In the meantime, I determined to use my eyes and ears as well as I could to find out the hidden facts, but so long as I possessed a friend in the house, I would be a fool not to use him and his information as well as I could. I was to attend Vidett on this day for the first time, and just after breakfast, he started out for a canter down the valley to see some friend in the town of San Marin, as he said. I went at his side, and behind us rode José and another among the riders. Vidett explained about them as we cantered along – he and I mounted upon splendid thoroughbreds and the two men on the wiry little horses which had set me such a dizzy pace across the mountains.

"We keep attendants always, as you see, Mendez," said Vidett. "Because, as Caporno has explained to you, of course, we exist in the midst of dangers constantly. These fellows are better fighters than you would guess. Although on their last trip they ran into one man who scattered four of them like chaff. However, Caporno has told you that story, of course."

I said that he had not.

"It was this Ames – this Hugo Ames. They have put fifteen thousand dollars reward on the head of that scoundrel, but he has gone four years without capture. However, you know a good deal about him?"

I told him that it was my business to find out about Ames. I only wondered why it was that Ames was an enemy of Lewis Vidett.

"Four of my servants," said Vidett, "started across the mountains on an errand. On their way back, this Ames fell foul of them. He scattered them like four handfuls of chaff. He killed one. But he is a stupid dolt, after all. They say that all criminals have weak spots in their minds. Instead of dropping a bullet through the head of the wounded man and taking out after the other two – whom he would have caught because they were almost frightened to death – he spent several weeks – imagine it if you can! – in taking care of the hurt man. Who, when he was healed, simply stole the mule of Ames –"

"Mule?" I exclaimed.

"Ah, you have not heard much of this Ames if you have not heard of his mule, Spike, which scales cliffs like a mountain goat. No horse can catch him through a course of rough country even when he has the bulk of his master on his back. His master is even larger than you are, Mendez! An inch or two taller. It is said that he weighs two hundred and fifty pounds! But this famous mule flaunts away under that enormous burden and beats the best of the horses over hard going. Hello!"

I do not use the stirrups much in riding, holding to the balance theory pretty thoroughly. But here my horse sidestepped with a violent bound and when I threw weight into the opposite stirrup the saddle suddenly gave way as though the girths were not binding in the slightest degree. I toppled onto the road.

It came near being the end of me. My fine thoroughbred turned suddenly into a devil. He began lunging and thrusting at me with forehoofs and with his teeth.

There was much shouting from the others, but it seemed to me that no one leaped in to my assistance as men should have done. It was only by chance, you may say, that an upward sweep of my hand managed to catch the reins beneath the chin of the horse. By that leverage I wrenched myself to my feet with such force that I almost broke the jaw of my horse at the same time.

That ugly man-killer was tamed the minute

he felt the force of my arm and stood like a lamb while the saddle, which was now under his belly, was righted. Then it was found that the girth had broken in two. José, with a strip of buckskin, proposed to remain behind and to sew the broken girth together again.

As for Vidett, he showed me the most extravagant concern, clapping me on the shoulder and swearing that it was the grace of heaven that had delivered me and that he would make the day a hot one for the groom who had permitted a girth to leave the stable in such a condition! In the meantime, he was late for his appointment in the town and he begged me to forgive him if he rode on and left me with José while he took the other rider with him.

I told him it was quite all right. There was nothing else that I could do, but it angered me to the heart to be shaken off his trail the very first day of my appointed guardianship. I had to stand by and watch José most expertly repair the damage which was done. But, first, I asked to see the break.

I examined the edges carefully. But they had not been cut. The ragged edges of the tear were sufficient evidence of that. When the damage was remedied, I swung into the saddle again, but before I started, I said savagely to José:

"Why do you have such a thoughtful look, José?"

He looked at me with his ugly grin which changed all at once to something like sunshine.

"Señor Ames – "

"Not that name!"

"Last night I was a dead man between your hands!"

"Well?"

"But I am still alive. You, señor, a moment ago were almost a dead man and – "

"At whose hands?"

José shrugged his shoulders; his eyes were speaking, but his tongue refused that duty.

"Look here, José," said I, "that girth was not cut."

"It was chafed very thin, however," said José. "And we all know that this horse is a man-killer when he gets his chance!"

It made the perspiration stand on my forehead.

"Vidett?" said I.

José nodded.

"Why in the name of the devil should he want to finish me? How am I a danger to him?"

"You follow him, señor!"

"To save his infernal hide!"

"Ah, señor, he wishes only to save himself. He does not wish to trouble others." His white

171

teeth flashed out at me.

"Very well," said I. "He wishes to have me out of his way, and in the meantime – but I cannot understand! The entire household is too much for me! José, how much do you know?"

"I, señor? Nothing, of course."

"There you are lying. But what do you guess, at least?"

"Will the señor ask me?"

"The marriage of Vidett and Señorita Rosa, for instance – if they are such lovers, why do they not marry and have that part of their troubles ended?"

José smiled on me with a savage meaning. "Perhaps it is not the wish of Señor Caporno."

"What?"

"I cannot tell. I guess. Suppose that they go to him and say, 'Tomorrow, or next week, we shall be married'? He only says to them: 'That is not wise, my children. I must bring all of my affairs into perfect order before this marriage takes place. So that all of my great fortune will be ordered and prepared for you.'"

A light darted upon my mind – a red light of danger, you may be sure!

"José, the old man does not wish this marriage in spite of all his talk about it?"

"It is not for me to read his mind," said José.

"He is opposed to it – he puts it off every day, all the time pretending that he wants nothing more than the immediate performance of the ceremony! That is it?"

"Señor, I cannot so much as guess!" But his grin assured me that I was right.

It suggested to me such a wild confusion of hatreds and shams in that apparently smooth household that I was more bewildered than I had been before I received that last bit of incredible information.

"Very well," said I. "Let us ride like the devil to catch up with them!"

We stormed along toward the town until a new thought made me draw heavily back on the rein and I brought my long-striding thoroughbred to a canter again. José had been distanced by that burst of racing speed, but now he drew up beside me again.

"If you ride in this manner, you will need a new horse every day, señor."

"Tell me, José. This Vidett is a man with many enemies, is he not?"

José laughed. "Ten thousand hate him!"

"Tell me, then, if you can guess, who is his greatest enemy in the world?"

"You, señor," said he.

"I am not speaking of myself. Who else?"

"Of the others – Señor Caporno! A child

could know that!"

Again I was so perfectly confused that my thoughts refused to function.

CHAPTER 20

I merely drove the spurs into the sides of my tormented horse and set him flying ahead at full speed. Here was growing up a problem so maddening that no one could make head or tail of it. Caporno hires for the protection of his household, but more particularly for the protection of his prospective son-in-law, the pseudo-Mendez. Now I learn, having taken the position, that Caporno desires nothing in the world so much as the death of this man! It was certainly enough to turn a feeble brain into a mad whirl. I was dizzy as I rode.

Before we reached the edge of the town of San Marin, however, I saw two horsemen swinging toward us, and they grew into the forms of Vidett and his attendant. Vidett, as he came up, seemed particularly full of cheer. He expressed the liveliest concern about my fall from the horse and prayed that such a thing would not happen again. I answered him as cheerfully as I could. I was afraid that, whatever the goal of his visit might have been, it was a thing which would not bode good for any one other than Vidett.

But on the rest of the ride back toward the house of Caporno, I kept silence. I was too busy with my thoughts, of course. It is foolish for me to rehearse this insane situation, because you will see the confusion of it as well as I did at that time. Perhaps you have already guessed the solution, though certainly no dream of a solution came to me. For, if Caporno wished the early death of Vidett, why he should hire a formidable guard for the person of that youth – but you see that this question becomes as baffling as the consideration of a first cause. It was quite beyond my comprehension.

Finally I determined that mere thinking could do me no good and that the best thing for me was simply to forget that I was in any tangle – keep my ears and eyes open – put two and two together when I was able – and never forget that the real objective of my visit to San Marin and my acceptance of a position in the house of Señor Caporno was the desire to discover the murderer of Truck Janvers.

After I had come to this conclusion, I felt much better, and I was beginning to enjoy the ride back up the valley. There was never a prettier place than that valley of the San Marin. It was lovely from the edges of the hills on either side; but it was prettiest of all when one rode near the bank of the river, with the clouds of willows along the edge and the silver glints of water showing through between the branches; and with scatterings of underbrush and trees on the farther side of the road.

We had just come in view of the wide roof lines of the house of Caporno itself when a voice barked from the side of the road: "Crinky!"

A word which had been haunting my ears like the name of an old friend, long unheard of!

I jerked around in the saddle, with a gun in either hand, and I saw a tall old man rising out of the brush with a rifle ready in his hand as he shouted. I heard a choked cry from Lewis Vidett as he whirled in the saddle, also, but he was late and wild with his shot. I knew that there was no time to waste, and as the butt of the tall fellow's rifle settled back in his shoulder, I tried a flying snapshot from the hip. The rifle spat out its fire and lead, but the big fellow was toppling before he pulled the trigger, and I did not have to look at Vidett to know that he was secure.

I drew rein and turned hastily back to the fallen body of the assailant among the brush.

I was late, however. Lewis Vidett himself was already there, flinging himself from the back of his horse with the activity of a wildcat.

I heard the fallen man cry: "Hold on, Crinky, you ain't gunna gut a man that's down –"

"You rat," said Crinky in snarling English – the first time I had heard him use that tongue, I think. "I'm going to send you home quick, Sam!"

"Crinky – for heaven's sake!"

"What chance did you give me? Here's the end of you, and perhaps after this –"

I heard this as I pressed up and hurled myself from my horse. But still I could not believe what I saw – one of the riders crouched on either side of the big, fallen man, holding his arms stretched out, and Lewis Vidett leaning over the prostrate figure with a revolver ready in his hand. I reached that hand and I drew it back, revolver and all.

Vidett jerked his head at me over his shoulder. What a face he showed me! All the sleeping devil was up in it – I mean his whole soul was showing, for there was nothing but devil in that man.

"Will you keep back from me, Mendez?"

"I'll not keep back from you if you mean to murder that fellow."

"Murder him?"

"I said that."

"After he tried to pot me out of the brush?"

"He sang out and gave you a fair warning."

Here the wounded man – he was bleeding freely, for my slug had cut him fairly through the center of one thigh – nodded happily to me.

"That's right, señor!" said he. For I had been talking Spanish out of sheer force of habit.

"This is good!" said Vidett, biting his lips with his fury. "Do I have to dispose of you before I can handle this skunk?"

Well, I had kept in my anger for quite a time, but now it was boiling in me, and I couldn't hold back any longer. I snapped the words back at him.

"You'll have to dispose of me," I assured him, "and that's something that you can't do, Señor Vidett."

"Stand to him, friend!" groaned the man Vidett had called Sam. "Stand to him, and the devil will wilt!"

Vidett's face quivered with fury. Then he cast a lightning glance down to his wrist, which was still in my grasp. I knew the reason of that glance. I had put my power into my fingers, and I knew that the right hand of Vidett would be numb and fairly useless for the next hour or so. No matter what his courage might be, he would have been a perfect fool to attack me with such a handicap working against him. He controlled himself with a frightful effort that made the perspiration come out in beads on his face and started his nostrils flaring.

"Ah, Mendez," he whispered to me, "what a fool you are to do this!" He added, aloud: "Very well. It was your shot that dropped him, and I owe you my life, perhaps, Mendez. Do with him whatever you choose to do. But I warn you that he's as dangerous and as treacherous as a rattlesnake!"

"We'll take him on to the house of Señor Caporno, of course," said I. "There's no better way, I suppose, of managing to take care of his wound."

Here Vidett flew into another rage, but a briefer one.

"Why in the name of the devil should his wound be cared for? Are you going to treat the dog like a Christian?"

I said no more to Vidett. I judged that I had crossed him sufficiently far in one day. But, with José and the other rider, we arranged a horse litter for the wounded man, slinging him very comfortably between two of the nags and then leading them at a gentle pace down the road.

"Friend," said Sam to me, "did I hear you say that you were taking me to the house of Caporno?"

"I am," said I in English.

"For heaven's sake stop here and put a slug through my head right now. It's what'll happen before the next morning comes!"

"Look here," said I. "You're going into that house under my protection. I'll be with you most of the time. If anything happens to you, they'll know that they're responsible to me."

He was in great pain which made his face pale, but as he looked up to me there was a twisting smile on his face. He stretched out his hand to me, and I closed mine over it with a nod of greater reassurance.

I was far from feeling that same assurance, however. Lewis Vidett was already flying down the road on his horse to tell his version of the encounter and of my actions to Señor Caporno. Here was I trailing in the rear, with no ability to arrange any lie to match against the inventions of Lewis Vidett. Besides, in such a game as this, I knew that he had much too great an intellectual subtlety for me to contend against him.

In the meantime, my heart was beating wild and high. For here was "Crinky," at last. It seemed like a dream of magic that I had been able to turn the name first found on the obscure letter in the hut of Truck Janvers into a living, breathing person.

But, at the same time, I felt that my problem was made more obscure than ever. For, having run this man down, I discovered that the man whom I suspected to be behind the death of Truck Janvers was the very one who had written a most submissively appealing letter to him. How could I reconcile these two ideas together?

However, I was fairly well past trying to link up every scrap in the evidence which was pouring so fast into my hands. It was enough that the trail of the murderer of Truck Janvers was growing hot and hotter to me. I trusted that the end of the trail was now not very far away!

When we reached the house of Caporno, a house *mozo* came hurrying out to us to tell us that a room had been arranged for the wounded man.

"As sure as my name is Sam Clyde," said the man on the litter, "I'll never live past tomorrow in that house of Caporno. Stranger, I give you my word for it!"

"Sam Clyde," said I, "if they murder you in my hands, they'll wish that they'd dropped a spark into a ton of dry powder. It will be quite a bit safer for them!"

He fastened one misty, pain-clouded eye upon me. Then he smiled faintly, as though the matter were so well settled in his mind that it was not worth the trouble of an argument — as though he thanked me, too, for my kindness to him.

CHAPTER 21

I gave Sam Clyde as much attention as I could, which was not much, for a wrinkle-faced Mexican Indian came in and dressed the wound in the thigh of Clyde, with more speed and thoroughness than I have ever seen before or since.

After Clyde had been made fairly comfortable, I sat beside him and asked him if there was anything that he wanted.

"The open sky to die under," said Clyde.

"You can't trust me?"

"Partner," said the other with a grin, "I make a point of trustin' any gent that sinks a chunk of lead in me fair and square the way that you done – a darn flippy and neat snapshot, it was. Well, sir, that's all very well. But you're one man in this house, and they got a-plenty more here. They might be sneakin' up behind my bed any time and ready to knife me in the dark as soon as you leave me."

I had to admit that there was that danger. That is to say, I had to admit it to myself, and even to him, tacitly, by the thing that I did next. I picked up the cot and the man in the cot and carried him to the corner of the room. He would not have such a stir of air about him, here, but he would at least have the security of a thick wall upon either side of him.

"Is that better?" I asked him.

He seemed much moved.

"Partner," said he, "You talk square, you shoot square, and I think that you are square. Then what you doin' mixed up with this bunch of hydrophobia cats?"

"Do you know a lot about them?" said I.

"I could talk a spell about 'em," he admitted.

"You'll talk to me, then?"

"Partner, are you kiddin' me? You mean to say that you're working for Caporno and that you don't really know him?"

"I suppose I have to admit that."

"Well," said he, "I'm darned!" And he lay staring at the ceiling.

I pushed the butt of a big Colt into his hand. He took it as though it were the hand of a friend in need and there was love in his eyes, I can tell you, as he looked down to it.

"Will that keep you company for a spell?"

"It'll keep me fine. So long, Mendez, if you got to leave me!"

I went straight to Caporno. He was enjoying a siesta and Pedro would not allow me to enter the room where he was sleeping. I took the dried-up little man beneath the armpits and lifted him out of the way. Then I stepped through the door and entered, leaving Pedro on the other side of the door, gasping and snarling like a sick old dog in the corridor.

The room was cool and dim. There was a feminine scent of perfume in the room. No, it was too strong to be merely feminine. It was Oriental. And there lay Caporno on a soft couch in the corner of the room. I could make out the huge silhouette of his belly against the wall. A water pipe stood near by. The rubber pipe that connected with it had slipped from the fat, inert fingers of Caporno, and he lay with mouth open, sleeping most unbeautifully.

I said: "Señor Caporno!"

It was exactly as though I had fired a pistol bullet into him. He leaped off the couch and shoved a heavy gun right under my nose, gasping: "Ah, murder!"

Then he saw that it was I, and it didn't seem to please him a great deal more. He stormed away into another rage and spilled quarts of fancy language all over the rug. He wanted to

186

know why I had come into his room while he slept. He wanted to know what I meant by it. How I had dared to come in, in spite of the prohibition which I must have received from Pedro at the door?

After he had run along for some time, I sat down on the arm of a chair and lighted a cigarette to show that I was willing to wait until he was tired before I would try to talk back. When he saw that, his temperature jumped another ten degrees and his language got so thick and so boiling in spite of its thickness, that I had to bring about a little halt.

I pointed my finger at him. "Señor," said I, "I am sorry to say that I have had enough!"

He blurted out half a dozen more triple-jointed insults and I cocked my finger again. I was pretty thoroughly angered. After four years of the life which I had led it may surprise you that mere language could have the slightest effect upon me. But it certainly did!

I said: "Caporno, if you curse me again, even a little one, even a 'damn,' I'll take you by the head and see what holds it to that fat neck of yours. That's final!"

He was instantly sobered. He sat down and snatched up a pipe. He sat cross-legged in the big chair he had selected and held the pipe like a Chairman and puffed furiously at it.

"What is it?" he asked me.

"I have brought a man named Sam Clyde into your house," said I. "Do you know him?"

"I never heard of him."

"Señor," said I, "I am afraid that is not true."

He took the pipe out of his mouth and blew a long, thin web of smoke against the ceiling of the room."

"So?" said he, without the slightest trace of heart.

"That is not true. You know a great deal about him, and so does he about you."

"Perhaps."

"He tells me that he cannot expect to live to see the morning in this house. Is there anything in that?"

"A great deal!"

"You expect to have him murdered?"

"Unquestionably. Do you object?"

"I do."

"I am sorry."

"If he dies before morning, you will be more than sorry. You will be very sad, señor."

"You speak with much strength – like a prophet, almost."

"There is very little difference," said I. "A prophet trusts in a dream or a vision or some such rot. I trust in my hands. They're worth a little trust."

I spread them out toward him and then clenched my fists and watched the rascal's eye and waited.

He appeared to debate the matter softly to himself, weighing the thing with a scrupulous scale that tottered back and forth a number of times. But, at length, he began to nod.

"I think it would be a considereable risk," declared he.

"It would," said I.

"I detest risks," said he. "You might even get at me. In case this Sam Clyde were to die before the morning, what would you have in mind concerning me?"

"Death, señor."

"Shocking," said Caporno, and grinned at me through a blue mist of pipe smoke. "You are engaged to serve me, in the meantime."

"I am, señor. But I have a thing called a sense of honor. It often comes between me and my work. I have never had glasses strong enough to let me look through it to what you would call the – facts!"

This was enough to have insulted almost any man. Well, it had not the slightest effect upon that Caporno. The villain wagged his head from side to side and chuckled at one of his thoughts.

"I love a man of honor," said he. "I have always liked to have them around me – for conversation. Sometimes, for use. Well, my friend, suppose that we strike a new little bargain regarding this?"

"Whatever you please."

I was so amazed by the easy fashion of my victory over him that I was ready to go to a great distance in any other respect in order to please him.

"This Clyde is a man of opinions and imagination. He might have a great deal to say about me; about Vidett, even. A very hard man in his language. Suppose that I agree that he shall not be injured in this house – will you agree not to listen to him if he were to try to talk?"

Another most odd proposal!

"Yes," said I.

"Then you are free to go back to him and tell him that his worries are ended. You will be expected to spend no more than thirty seconds in his room. You understand me?"

"Exactly."

"Adios. Watch for Pedro at the door as you go out. He is apt to try to knife you because I suppose that you used force on him."

Old Pedro would certainly have planted his knife between a pair of my ribs had it not been for this timely warning. As I stepped cautiously through the doorway, looking to either side,

I made out Pedro, flattened against the wall on my right, flattened until he seemed rather a bas-relief than a man. He jabbed at me with a knife and I had barely time to knock his hand up. Then I whirled him around and tossed him into the room of his genial master and immediately closed the door gently after him.

I felt as if I had had my hands on the body of an old snake in which the poison is dried but the fangs are still sharp. Then I went to see Sam Clyde. I found him lying on his back, combing his long yellow mustaches, with a frown on his sun-blackened face. I was greeted with a leveled revolver, which was lowered the instant he recognized me.

"Well?" said he.

I went to him and took the revolver out of his hand.

"You are safe," said I, "as long as I am safe. Do you understand? They will not knife you or poison you until they have disposed of me. Will that do for you?"

He scanned me again and then fumbled for my hand and found it. "Partner," said he, "I begin to hope. I got to say –"

"I've no time to listen. I'm under honor not to talk to you while you're in the house. I'll look in at you once every day. So long!"

"God bless you!" said he, and I left the room.

CHAPTER 22

Old Caporno was standing down the hall, staring at me, as I issued from the doorway, and his watch was in his hand.

"Just five seconds over," said he.

"I thought you were using a figure of speech," said I.

"When I make a bargain," said he, "I never use figures of speech. However, this is all right. I think that you're still honest, Mendez."

He came up to me and linked his fat arm in mine almost affectionately.

"Very well," said he, "for so long as you remain fairly honest, I am fairly disposed to keep you with me. It is a bargain, is it not?"

"Of course. Who is to be judge?"

"Either of us. I am sorry to hear that you have had troubles with Vidett."

"Has he told you about it?"

"Yes."

"What has he told you?"

He paused and frowned a little in thought.

"The truth, I think. Yes, I believe that he has told me nothing but the truth. Lies from him to me or from me to him are so difficult ˍ that eventually they are really not worth while, if you can understand what I mean by that!"

I understood that I was in an atmosphere filled with poison and with daggers.

"I can understand," said I. "You heard the truth, then, you think?"

"I did."

"What did you make out of it?"

"I don't know what you mean."

"Which of us was right?"

"Right? I rarely bother with such matters. Ethics is a science with which I have had very little to do. But what I usually strive after are the ascertained facts. You follow me? I wish to know what has happened, rather than what might have happened, or the reason behind."

I nodded. Yet it was a viewpoint difficult for me to grapple with.

"What is of importance is that you saved the life of Mr. Vidett. A moment later, you mortally offended him. Which, I suppose, more or less counterbalances the first service."

"So that I remain with him exactly as though today had never come between us? One thing has neutralized the other?"

Caporno grinned sharply aside at me, and, stopping the shuffling of his slippers, he slapped one of them violently against the floor.

"Excellent!" said he. "I am delighted by that. I tell you, my amiable Mendez, that if you were dealing with me directly in this matter of today, that would be exactly my attitude concerning it. This, however, is different. In Vidett, you have to deal with a man of brilliancy, but not of judgment. His brain is at present under the cloud of prejudice which you raised in it a little time ago. I am sorry."

"At present, then, he is an enemy?"

Caporno made a gesture of surrender.

"Well," said I, "while I guard him, I shall do my very best to guard against him!"

Caporno actually sighed. "Yet," said he, "in a way it must be delightful – to an adventurous young spirit like yours."

"Señor," said I, "I have been four years –"

But here I paused, for it would not do to give him details out of my life which might connect me in his mind with my true identity.

"Four years of what?"

"Of the truest hell!" I admitted to him. "So that I really am not very eager for more trouble. This is – "

"A business venture?"

"Yes. Call it that."

Caporno turned upon me and took my hand. "You are in a position of the greatest difficulty," said he, bowing toward me a little. "I trust that you will solve the problem."

In this fashion that unique fellow parted from me. But events had become so strange and so strangely crowded in the house of Caporno, that I no longer paid much attention to little matters such as those through which I had just passed.

I went back to my own room and threw myself down on my bed for a moment of rest and of reflection – mental rest was what I most needed. But I felt as though I had drunk too much. The moment I lay down, my head began to spin. I started up again, and I hurried as fast as I could to find Mr. Lewis Vidett.

He was in the open yard behind the garden and in front of the corrals, and he was talking busily with two or three of the riders, who listened with the greatest gravity to what he had to say.

I came straight up to him, with my mind made up.

"Vidett –" said I as I came near.

He turned on me without a word, but with a slight paling of his color which told me how truly he hated me for the offense which I had given him.

"I have come, señor," said I, bowing to him, "to tell you that I realize that I was unpardonable in laying a hand upon you – and to beg you to forgive me!"

I said this loudly, so that the riders would be sure to hear me, for I was rather sure that one reason the rascal hated me was, because I had mastered him in the presence of witnesses. He was shocked by this address of mine into an audible gasp. Then I saw his bright eyes flicker to one side and to the other, drinking with infinite satisfaction the expressions which he found upon the faces of the riders – expressions of surprise and contempt.

Of course they were thinking that I made this apology owing to fear of him. I suppose that it would have torn the heart of most men to allow even a servant to have such disdainful thoughts concerning him. But, for my part, I did not care a whit at that moment what any one in the world thought of myself – except the people who were most intimately connected with me.

Then I heard Vidett saying slowly, with relish: "I was afraid that I would have to speak to you again on this subject –"

"I trust it is finished now," said I, still more humble than before.

"I think that you have said enough," said Vidett in a lordly fashion, and he held out his hand to me with the air of a duke to his lowest retainer.

I stepped closer, and as I took that hand I murmured behind a smile: "I have set you right in the eyes of these men, Vidett. But I know that you hate me in your heart, and in my heart I want you to know that I detest you for a poisonous dog!"

His self-control was so miraculous that he received this fairly stinging speech with a sudden almost happy lifting of his eyes and a bright smile upon me.

"Really?" said he. "You intrigue me, Mendez."

He drew me aside a few paces. We continued to smile for the benefit of the sharp-eyed watchers.

"You mean it?" said he.

"With all my heart."

"What has made you hate me?" he asked, with a sort of idle curiosity.

"I don't know, frankly," said I. "Your wish to kill a helpless man while your two riders held his arms — that was something, but still it was not enough for the feeling which I have in my heart about you. I trust that you will understand me?"

"It is an instinctive loathing?" he asked merrily.

"You have it, exactly."

"My dear friend, we can now speak for one another. I abhor you from my soul."

"I ask you for what reason?"

"The best reason that can be found in the entire world – because you have dared to look down on me and scorn me! You must pay me for that!"

"I shall do that to the best of my ability."

"Until that happy time, adios."

"Adios. I shall do my best to continue to guard you from harm!"

"Swine of a Spaniard," said Vidett through his smile.

CHAPTER 23

I went back to Caporno and told him that his son-to-be and I were at least upon a pseudo-friendly footing – that we had given up attempts at deceit and were frank with each other. Caporno listened to me with an elflike smile that foreboded mischief. On the way back, I peeked into the room of old Sam Clyde – who knew the things which Caporno was so anxious that I should not know! He winked and waved at me, and I smiled and waved at him. Then I went back to Vidett.

I remained with him through the day. Where he went, I followed. Though I could see that he resented this close attendance intensely, I kept at his side. In the middle of the afternoon, however, he told me that I should not be needed for an hour or more, because he was about to interview Rosa and her father privately. I told him that I was extremely sorry.

That I should be glad to keep out of earshot of the party, but that I must certainly remain near enough to keep my eye upon them.

Vidett listened to me with a sort of incredulous rage. Then he turned his shoulder on me and strode for the house. I followed at his heel, grinning to myself. When he reached Caporno he demanded in a voice of iron whether or not I were appointed to dog his footsteps everywhere. Caporno's answer was as smooth and as deft as I had expected.

"In the name of heaven, dear Lewis, what will you have me do? Let you risk your life?"

"This is a matter for the three of us, surely," said Vidett.

"My dear boy, I have nothing to say to you which I shall not be glad to have any man of honor overhear!"

I listened to this tale with much amusement, and with dread also, for I had no real desire to push the rage of Vidett past a certain point.

"Very well, then," said Vidett at last, "let him stay in the same room with the three of us."

"As you wish!" said Caporno.

That was why I remained in the chamber of Caporno when his daughter came in to consult with him and with Lewis Vidett. I was withdrawn to the farthest corner of the room, of course. But still it was very noticeable that Rosa stopped short and stared when she first noticed me.

"I have resolved to keep the guard of Lewis' safety constantly with him," said her father.

Rosa thanked him, but I thought that her smile was rather wry. "I suppose this is to make the talk short – and not to the point," said she.

"Not at all," said Caporno. "My dear child, speak freely before Mendez. Any gentleman is welcome to overhear whatever is in mind."

His daughter bit her lip, and then she tossed up her head. "Since you are here, Señor Mendez, will you join our circle?"

I told her that I preferred remaining where I was, because I desired to watch Vidett, but not at all to eavesdrop upon what they said to one another.

"Dear Father," sneered Rosa, "you are so thoughtful of the safety of my Lewis! But as for secrecy, I care about it as little as you do. You know why I begged for this last interview. For the last time I want to beg you to give in to us; we wish to be married immediately! For the thousandth time, Father, tell us why do you hold out against us?"

"Rosa," said her father, "I have promised to let you speak for the last time of this affair. It ought to be enough for you that I do not approve of the marriage at present. It is not a matter which has anything to do with Lewis. You know my preference for him!"

"I know the preference which you pretend!" said Rosa.

If I had thought her hard before, she was like flint now. I have never listened to a less feminine woman. Her voice rose with a bold ring that filled the room. I could have heard her if I had covered my ears.

"Child, child," said Caporno, adopting melting tones, "you do not understand! How could I have any wish other than the greatest happiness for the two of you?"

"Heaven alone knows what goes on in your head!" said the girl, meeting his eye fairly and squarely.

At least, I had to admire her courage. All the time, from the distance, I was admiring the exquisite slender, girlish beauty of the daughter of Caporno. I was admiring that beauty and seeing more and more that in such a child he was punished for all his sins, no matter how many they might be!

"Very well," said the father. "I tell you for the thousandth time that I cannot conduct the affairs of my life as common men do. There is a certain diplomacy which is necessary. Some of my affairs are in confusion and for the present –"

"You have told us that for six months," cried the girl in a fury.

"It is true, nevertheless."

"Señor," broke in Vidett, speaking for the first time, "I entreat you now to name a day."

"A day? Do you wish that?"

"We do."

"Shall I say, then – two months from today?"

"Two months!"

"Is that too long?"

"Eternity!"

"But, my children, there are such matters as trousseaus –"

"They matter nothing at all to us."

"You are determined, then?"

"Perfectly!"

"Very well – only one month."

"One eternity!"

They both cried this in a single voice.

"In two weeks from today, then, Rosa."

"It is too long. We have waited forever, already!"

"In what time do you suggest?" asked the father coldly.

"Tomorrow!" cried Rosa.

"Impossible."

"In a week from this day, señor," suggested Vidett more courteously.

"In a week, then," said Caporno. "But you wring my heart with your haste!"

He might better have said: "You fill me with wild fury with your haste!" I, never moving my eyes from that fat face of his, saw the strength of his emotion. Then I followed the girl and her lover from the room. I knew that this was a grim decision which had been forced from Caporno, and I knew that he was ready to strike and to strike hard at his son-in-law.

Vidett, as soon as he was alone in the corridor with Rosa — save for me, following in the little distance — turned his head sharply over his shoulder and barked at me: "Señor Mendez, keep your distance, if you please!"

I fell back an obedient distance, and they continued talking together rapidly, the girl filled with joy over the victory which she had extorted from her father, and Lewis Vidett shaking his head and very grave. At length this gravity of his began to prove more contagious. Once or twice she half turned and threw back glances of distrust at me, glances rapidly darkening! The eye of no man has ever given me such fear as did the glance of this girl!

Then she seemed to argue with him; I heard him say: "I am afraid of your father, Rosa."

That was all I actually overheard.

They broke off their talk and suddenly came

back to me, Rosa smiling very happily.

"We have talked everything over," she said, holding out her hand, "and I am apologizing for Lewis because he has treated you in such a manner. Because I, señor, know that the man who saved his life cannot be his enemy, really! I have persuaded Lewis to trust you. Will you in turn trust me, and him?"

Of course there was nothing for me to do but to thank her and tell her that in everything I should hope to do as she and Vidett wished. Beyond that, I desired their happiness, I told them, in the match the plans for which I had overheard. Vidett now gripped my hand with a fine strength, and I felt rather ashamed of all the suspicions which had been so dark in my mind a few moments before. During the rest of that day I was with Vidett, not as a spy or a guard, but as a friend. He chattered away merrily, asking me a thousand questions, and when I would not talk, he unbosomed himself and told me tales out of his own life.

True stories – of gambling, mostly. Though his part in the stories was dexterously white-washed so as to be fairly clean, yet one could see the rascal that he was peeping out from behind every bush, so to speak. No, I did not like Vidett a whit better for his talk and his friendliness of that day, but I had to admit that he was infinitely entertaining.

He was particularly attentive to me and cordial during the lunch and the dinner hours. Caporno, passing me after the dinner was ended, whispered softly:

"Beware!"

That was all, and it was enough. As though he had cupped cold water in his hand and dashed it into my face. I retired and decided that I must be on my watch. I should beware of only one thing, naturally – Vidett!

However, I could see nothing wrong. After dinner, we sat in the garden, for a time, and Rosa strummed a guitar and created a real music out of the strings. Vidett sat near her and sang a soft high baritone, with tenor notes taken deftly in falsetto. While I watched the stars, and the dark tops of the trees against them until Vidett stood up to go to bed – at the same time the snore of Caporno announced that he was sleeping. I went in with Lewis Vidett, and before I started for my own room, he called me back.

"To pledge our new friendship, my dear friend!"

He poured out two glasses of a heady, spiced wine, and we drank to one another. I remember the flash of his teeth as he smiled when I bade him good night. There was that one similarity between him and his betrothed – their strange, quick, mirthless smiles. But, when I had turned the lock of my bedroom door, a wave of blackness struck across my brain, and I realized suddenly that there had been a reason for the smile of Vidett!

CHAPTER 24

Of course I knew that it was a knock-out drop or a fatal poison. I was fairly well decided that it was only a knock-out drop, however, for I did not believe that even Lewis Vidett would dare to aim a greater stroke at a man hired by Caporno. I wanted an emetic and I wanted it badly. In the meantime, I was sinking under a weight of those black waves which started at my feet and went shooting toward my head.

I opened that door with a hand already growing numb. I hurried down the passage, thanking heaven that the nerves of my legs were still unaffected. I reached the kitchen and asked a frightened *mozo* for mustard and hot water. A glass of that pungent mixture was placed in my hand, and I went with it out into the night.

There is no emetic which is much better. I don't want to go into that disagreeable subject; I'll simply say that I was pretty thoroughly rinsed before I finished drinking that glass of mustard and hot water.

Then I lay on my face in the clean sand of the garden path and felt the coolness of the night working slowly at the heat of my forehead and the thrumming of little hammers at my temples and at the base of my brain. Still, I had to use all the force of my will to drag myself stiffly to my feet, and I was staggering drunkenly – not because my body was affected, but because everything whirled before my eyes and the stars turned into bright individual streaks of white fire across the face of the night.

Then, rapidly – because I had the stuff out of me before a great deal of it got into my system – I righted. I knew where I was, what I was doing, and that I had to find the trail of my friend, Lewis Vidett, and find it at once.

First of all, however, I could not start without guns, and my gun belt was in my room. I hurried back for it. I knew where it hung, and I extracted the weapons from it in the darkness and shoved them into my clothes. I was doing that when I heard a soft step pause in the hall outside my door.

Any child might have guessed that the stealthy footfall did not belong to any friend of mine. I could put that down easily enough.

But who was it, then? Vidett, or one of his cut-throats, come back to make out whether or no I were really peaceably asleep under the influence of the drug.

When I guessed that much, the rest was easily done. I reached the side of the bed with one stride, and I covered the noise of my heavy body sinking on the mattress and the springs with a big groan. A sleepy, half stifled groan – of the kind that a thick sleeper will use!

In another instant I was cursing myself profoundly, for I heard a hand stealthily trying the door. If they wanted to come in and have a look at me, it was too bad that they couldn't do it. I was only too willing to sham absolute sleep for them. However, I had turned the lock of the door as I reentered.

My regret ended. A little matter such as a turned lock did not matter, it appeared, in this house. I heard, now, a busy little clinking sound of metal against metal; then the door softly opened and a draft crossed my room, from window to door, with a ghostly, sighing whisper.

A rustle, a stir, and a shadow leaned over me with the familiar glint of steel in a ready hand. For I recognized the glimmer of steel as an Italian stiletto, and the dim face above the knife was that of Lewis Vidett. Perhaps he preferred to know that I was harmlessly asleep. But, in case there were any doubt, he was determined at least that I should not follow him on this night! Admirably thorough indeed was Lewis Vidett!

He brought something else into his other hand and then a stream of light flared across my face!

I was prepared for anything other than an electric torch. That blinding brilliancy ate through the skin of my eyelids and spread a crimson dawn before my eye. Endure it without at least twitching my eyelids I could not. So I stretched my entire body, groaned heavily, turned from him bodily, and then relaxed every muscle of my body with a slump and another sigh.

Lewis Vidett leaned over me still farther and shone the torch against my face. Through the lashes of my eyes I could see him. And to have that man behind me – well, it was a good deal more terrible than having the eyes of a panther stealing up from the rear. I could feel the heart tighten and my muscles contracting. I could not endure it another moment without whirling on him – and getting that slender tongue of steel buried in my body!

But when the breaking point had come with

me, he snapped out the flood of blazing light. He had, apparently, seen enough to satisfy him that I was not feigning sleep. I blessed him for that conclusion.

"Well, little Mendez," he said, making no effort to keep his voice low, "sleep heartily — sleep soundly! Even the mustard and the water could do no more than give you a perfumed sleep — so it seems!"

He went, softly chuckling, from the room.

I had exactly the feeling that a wildcat had left me, as the door closed behind him. I was about to start quietly from the bed when the door jerked open again, and a steady shaft of light from the electric torch probed for me — I settled myself in that instant! — and found me exactly as I had been before. Perhaps some air-borne suspicion had come to the sensitive brain of Vidett. At least, I will assure you that that ray of light went through me more terribly than a bullet.

But, when the door was closed that second time, I felt that even the suspicions of a Vidett must be thoroughly appeased by what he had seen. I counted ten — twice. Then I got up and started in pursuit. Not through the door. No, I did not want to trust myself to hinges which may creak. I was behind the lines — in the enemies' territory with a vengeance. First of all, I wanted to get onto neutral ground. To get there, I leaped through the window and slid off into the garden, where I knelt behind a hedge with my two eyes multiplied into ten, at the least!

There was danger. Oh, it was in the air. It came like a bitter wine into my blood. Danger, danger! I knelt there quivering and thoroughly frightened, with a gun in my hand, ready for anything.

But what I saw was only the meager silhouette of one man leaving the house of Caporno.

One man, but by his springing, active step I knew him. It was Lewis Vidett!

I went after him at once. No, not exactly after him. My experience has taught me that a fellow has better chances of remaining undetected if he pursues a little to the side. For a suspicious man will nearly always, when he hears a sound, whirl about and look first straight behind him. Lewis Vidett was indeed a most suspicious man!

Every one of his nerves – on this occasion at the least – seemed to be mounted upon a hair trigger. A dozen times I melted into the ground behind some shrub or tree trunk. A dozen times he went on again.

He went straight on, at length, into the

woods, and there I was forced to walk at full speed, cursing the boots which were on my feet, and cursing even the breath which I had to draw. The flutter of a very shadow was all that was needed to warn the cat who stalked ahead of me.

However, I managed to keep softly behind him. Just as I was beginning to perspire and despair, I had my reward. Vidett, stepping from behind a big tree into a little moon-dimmed clearing among the trees, suddenly tilted up his head and whistled three times, softly.

For answer, a round score of men started out from the trees! Twenty men! And each man with weapons belted around his hips, and each man with a mask thrown over his face. I had never seen it before. It thickened my blood, I can tell you, to see those black faces under the dull moon!

They gathered hastily around young Lewis Vidett, and I could see that they were heartily glad to have met with him. There was a great shaking of hands, in the first place, so that it set up a jingling of guns – a faint, stern, humming noise, as you might call it.

After that, they put their heads together and there was a conference. It lasted for perhaps ten or fifteen minutes, and I wriggled as close as I dared. I got close enough to find that these fellows were all so thoroughly masked and hooded that there was not the slightest chance that I could make out any features. I got close enough to make out an occasional exclamation, always in Spanish, and an occasional "Señor!"

Once I heard a man say: "For the republic –"

Well, it was enough for me, at the moment. I mean to say that it was enough to fix in my mind that there was trouble brewing and that it probably had to do with the business dealings between Caporno and his deserted republic – which he had made good by the very excess of his personal wickedness, according to him. That was the matter on account of which they should be grateful to him!

More than one fist and more than one weapon was brandished toward the house of Caporno. I felt that it was the merest folly to wait any longer. My place was back in the house. The twenty were surely enough protection for Señor Vidett!

So I cut for the house, and I cut fast. I tore off my boots with a force that almost broke my ankles, and I slid along at full speed as soon as I was out of what you might call whispering distance of them. I tore for the edge of the woods, first, and then I doubled back across the open and traveled by way of the shrubs and the hedges, looking back fifty times to make sure that I was not being followed.

It is a wonderful thing how terror leaps into your heart the moment you turn your back and run. I've often wondered how a whole army of brave men could be routed. But that night I understood. I ran so wildly and so fast that I felt like charging straight past the house of Caporno. Twenty murderers were somewhere in the night behind me. I felt as though each of them were gliding straight after me, now, fleet as the wing of a skimming owl.

I got to the side door. It was locked, of course. I plunged, panting, around the side of the building and then clambered up through the window into my own room. Even there the fear did not abate. I crouched against the floor with my heart thundering. In every corner of the room I seemed to see quivering outlines of approaching assassins.

CHAPTER 25

I tell you how I lay shuddering in a corner of my room, too much unmanned to stand up and give the warning which should be given, so that you may understand how much the devilish nature of Vidett had worked upon me.

I rallied myself after a moment, and I hurried out of my room into the hallway. I ran to the end of it and looked across the field beyond the house. The trees made a background against which it was hard to distinguish anything. But, after a moment, I thought that I saw dim forms beneath the moon stealing out from the verge of the copse.

That determined me. I ran for the door of Caporno's room and rapped at it.

There was no answer.

I called softly, and then more loudly: "It is I! Mendez! Very urgent news, Caporno."

The second time I repeated this so loudly that

I thought I heard an empty echo mocking me from within the room of the lord of the house, and that alarmed me. I knocked heavily once more, and then as there was not a stir in answer from within, I gave the door my shoulder.

It was like pressing my hand against a wall. There was no response. I ran back the width of the hall and turned myself into a battering ram, using the thick cushion of muscle at the point of my shoulder as the point of impact. Two hundred and twenty pounds of driving bone and muscle crunched the wood of the door through the iron of the lock and with a great tearing and ripping sound, almost like that of parting cloth, the door came wide and I stumbled into the chamber and tripped over a form lying just across the passage from the threshold.

There was a lamp standing on a table in a corner of the room, but it was turned down so low that it gave me no light to aid me in my work. I looked wildly around me. What I had to show me my way was the shaft of the moonlight which spilled dreamily through the two great, tall casements at that side of the master's room.

First of all, here was the form on the floor over which I had lurched.

I scooped up a light, thin body, and carried

it into the light. It was Pedro. His old, sagging mouth had fallen ajar; his eyes were lost in black hollows beneath his brows. His ancient skin was waxy white, a horrible sight, and from his lips I scented the familiar and detestable fragrance of the spiced wine with which I myself had been so nearly drugged on that night.

Pedro lived, indeed, but he was as good as dead.

I tossed him lightly onto a deep couch where he usually slept, for he never left the room of Caporno. Then I hurried on to the great four-posted bed. As I leaned inside the drapery, I had my answer readily supplied to me. It was the same hateful perfume of that half-poisoned wine with which Vidett had apparently been dosing the entire household on this night.

However, I was now desperate. I could not help remembering that I had fought off the effects of the potion for myself. I picked up the great, loose body of Caporno and dragged him to the edge of the bed. I turned up the flame in the throat of the lamp.

He had been so heavily drugged that his face was ghastly to behold and his entire body was quivering – lightly and steadily. I remembered now what José had told me – that Vidett hated Caporno and Caporno hated Vidett. I could believe that story. Yet it seemed madness that Vidett should have struck such a blow at the father of the girl he was to marry! No matter for what purpose, Vidett was not the sort of a man to let love lead him into financial losses, and if he offended the excellent Caporno, the vast fortune of which Caporno was said to be the master was lost to him!

I took Caporno's head between my hands and I ground the knuckles into his forehead until I felt the bone fairly sag beneath the force of my grip. Then I dragged those knuckles slowly across his head.

There was a groan and a convulsive stir almost at once in answer to this torment. I continued. There was a gasping voice:

"Who – oh, Lord!" And a fat, cold hand caught at my wrist.

I saw that the troubled, misted eyes of Caporno were opened and staring up at me.

"Caporno!" I snarled in his ear. "Vidett is coming – with twenty men!"

There was no slightest sense of my meaning in his features. I struck him brutally across the face. At that, he made a feeble attempt to strike me, and his fat hand rebounded from my shoulder.

"Vidett – coming for the house – with twenty men – speaking of a republic – Vidett

– twenty men – coming for you!"

Gradually, with brutal violence and with words like knife stabs, I had roused him. No, he was not altogether out of the blaze, but one flash of semi-consciousness came back to him. He moved his lips as though to say that he understood what treacherous artifice had been used to incapacitate him for the night.

"The cellars!" said Caporno. "The keys!" And he strove to reach under the pillow of his bed.

I slid my own hand under it and brought it out and showed him my empty palm.

What a convulsion of the face rewarded me as he saw! Still the drug was fighting heavily to overcome him once more. He battled like a dying man to regain his senses. But the battle was lost before it was well begun.

"Vidett!" he murmured at my ear. "He has drugged – taken the keys – the cellars – for heaven's sake."

I shook him violently, holding him by handfuls of his soft flesh and bruising it to a miserable pulp beneath my fingers.

"Caporno – what in the cellars?"

He tried to speak. His flabby, empurpled lips moved violently, but they gave forth only an unintelligible jargon. I saw the light beginning to fade from him once more.

He was sinking back in the coma once again but now, as I leaned over him, I heard him whisper: "Rosa!"

It was only the faintest murmur, and spoken at such a time, I suppose that I might as well have considered it an instinctive appeal to her to come to his help. But I would as soon have turned for help to an ogress, so perfectly did I distrust and detest that cold-faced girl!

I said to myself that I was beaten, now. For, already they would be advancing close to the house. Rosa? Beyond a doubt she was merely waiting for the coming of her lover. What was her father to her? I looked upon her as simply a she-devil!

Yet it seemed more than odd that she should have been named by Caporno. He was not a fool. Even as he was sinking back into a poisoned dream, it seemed most likely that he would not guide me into wrong hands so long as I was working in his interests.

I stood for a moment with my hands gripped hard and my breath coming fast, and my thoughts spinning dizzily. I remember that a great artery in the side of my throat was flurrying with an irregular beat, sending stabs of pain into my brain.

So I turned with a sudden clearing of doubts. It might not be the wise thing to do, but it was

222

all that remained. I knew that I could not stand idly!

I whipped out of the chamber of Señor Caporno and I raced for the upstairs, where I knew that I could find the chamber of Rosa. I knew that because it had been pointed out to me – by the little balcony which extended beneath her three windows – windows and balcony all covered with trailing vines, and the vines starred over with tiniest white blossoms.

From the main hall I came to a French door which opened upon that balcony. It was not locked, by lucky chance. I opened that door and stepped onto the balcony. Below me lay the patio, its pavement painted white by the moon, and the still-tossing spray casting a delicate and wavering tracery of shadow across the flags, near the fountain pool.

That was not all I saw. For I marked four men, running on padded feet, that sounded like a dim trampling through the soft, lush grass of spring. They were leaning far forward with their furtive speed as they darted across the patio, leaping into the emblossoming shade on the nearer side just beneath me.

What was their goal? My room? The room of Caporno? The cellars for which Caporno trembled so much?

Or were they at that moment racing up to

the bedchamber of their confederate's lover, to take her away with them, or to ask for her final help in the directions for the plundering of the house. For that, I decided, was what the guilty pair must have had in mind. They did not dare to trust that Caporno would live up to his word and would allow them to marry freely at the end of the week. They had decided to end him on the spot and scoop up the money which was in his house.

Here was I, his hired guard – his body servant – standing with idle hands! I have rarely passed through such a vital instant of agony.

But then I ran out onto the balcony and reached the three windows of the chamber of Rosa, wondering always, what eyes of skulkers from the patio beneath me might mark me there. I called through the open window: "Señorita Caporno!"

There was no answer.

I pried the window open to its full height. "Señorita Caporno!"

There was a frightened gasp: "Ah! Who is it? Señor Vidett?"

It was not the voice of Rosa. I would wait no longer. From the patio beneath me at that very instant a gun might be training on me. I dragged myself through the window and stood within the room.

There I saw the bed — tall and old-fashioned and four-posted, like the bed of Caporno, and a dark-haired face on the pillow. And beside the bed, clutching at her mistress and shaking her to wake her, and with a terrified head turned toward me, I saw by the dim moon the little frightened maid of Rosa Caporno. I did not need to stir from where I stood. For, by the eternal heavens, a stir of wind brought me what I had breathed too often before on that night — the heady fragrance of the spiced wine!

CHAPTER 26

I reached that bed in a leap which frightened the servant almost into a swoon, and leaning over the face of her mistress I knew by the parted lips and the pallor that my first surmise had been the perfectly correct one.

Then I turned back to the maid. She was on the verge of a collapse; half courageous and ready to save her mistress from me; half a coward and wanting to flee; but too weak with fear to do either.

I picked her up with one arm, planted her on a couch, and turned up the flame of a lamp on a little table beside it. There is nothing like a bit of light to knock fear into a cocked hat.

"Now," said I to her, "what has happened to you?"

She had a fist pressed against each cheek, gaping at me as though I were apt to eat her the next instant.

I decided to give her the spur as hard as I could.

"There are twenty armed men rummaging through this house," said I. "Is that door locked?"

"With a bolt!" said the girl very quickly.

She reacted as women very often do – wilting at the first sign of trouble, and then growing stronger when they see that there is a real crisis ahead. Now she sat up straighter and watched me with less dread and enmity.

"I am your friend – the friend of the señorita – tell me who gave her that drug? That poison?"

At the last word she uttered a faint little cry. "Poison!"

"It is a drugged wine that was given to her."

"How do you know that?"

"Do you know it, too?"

"God have mercy – is my beautiful lady to die?"

"She will live. But what happened? Who gave her the wine?"

"I cannot tell."

"Was it Vidett?"

At this her eyes popped wider, as though I were reading this stuff out of her mind.

"Señor!" she gasped.

"I know it must have been Vidett," said

I. "But what happened first? Was there a quarrel?"

"Yes."

The word broke from her and then she clapped her hand over her mouth.

"Listen, little fool!" said I, and I put on her wrist a grip that was a hundred pounds too heavy. "I am the friend of the señorita. What happened?"

Then speech tumbled out of the girl in a flood. She told me everything she knew. It was so confused that I had to pick my way among the fragments and the ruins and the suggestions and the exaggerations of facts.

Lewis Vidett had come to see the lady of his heart on the little balcony outside her windows. He on the balcony, she within the windows, they had chattered with one another for some time, and the little *moza*, in the obscurity of the room, knew that her mistress was being persuaded by Vidett – persuaded toward what, she could not tell. At length, Señor Vidett rose up with a furious exclamation and flung away from Rosa Caporno.

As for Rosa, she herself was in a tantrum, but her anger melted almost at once. She began by scolding her poor *moza* and then by weeping upon her shoulder, and finally she had thrown herself on the bed, face down, and had sobbed heavily.

A moment later, the step of a man on the balcony and the familiar figure of Vidett leaning at the window – for the French doors were locked. He called to Rosa, who refused to come, at first, but then he persuaded her and told her that he had brought up a glass of spiced wine so that they could drink a happy good night to one another – a sort of sleeping cup!

Rosa had stood up and gone to him, at this. He had kissed her, and given her the cup and pledged her, and after she had drunk, she went back to her bed and lay down and was instantly asleep – without pausing to take off her clothes.

The *moza* watched her eagerly. Finally, as the time wore on, she ventured to disturb her mistress, but she could not rouse her to more than a moan. After that, she became frightened. She noticed the heavy scent of the wine which still filled the chamber. She herself had thought of poison, and yet it had seemed too impossible, for the quarrel between the pair had been neither long nor violent.

In the end, after listening to the heart of her mistress and finding that its beat was steady and fairly strong, she had made up her mind to wait until she slept off the effects of the drugged potion, for she had wit and experience enough to guess that this was the cause of the heavy slumber.

I had learned enough from the maid by this time. I told her instantly to draw a tubful of water, and she did not disobey nor ask questions. I presume that the young tyrant, her mistress, had schooled her in ready obedience!

I heard the grand rushing of the water in the bathroom and I knew that such a tap would fill the tub in a moment. I went straight to the bed of Rosa Caporno and lifted her in my arms. She was so perfectly limp with sleep that it was difficult to keep hold on her. She seemed to be melting through my arms. But, at length, she was against my breast, legs and arms and head dangling, and I carried her into the adjoining bathroom.

The *moza* uttered a frightened gasp, and then she nodded in comprehension. The tub was filled to the brim; the water turned off; and then I swayed Rosa bodily beneath the surface of the water. It cast out a great wave that drenched me to my knees; and Rosa came gasping and sputtering up to the surface.

Perhaps her lover had given her a smaller dose than that with which he had stunned the faculties of her father, Pedro, and me. However, there she was awake in a moment, shuddering with cold, her wet clothes clinging to her body, her teeth chattering, and her eyes wide and bright with wonder as she watched me.

The *moza* began to whisper explanations at her ear. She pushed the girl away. She said to me with a wonderful calmness and courage: "You are in my sleeping room, señor. Has my father sent you here?"

No reproaches, no screams, no exclamations, though her brain must have been reeling with the violence of the drug at that moment.

I said simply: "Señorita, your father could not have sent me to you, because he is lying on his bed at this moment, drugged as I found you drugged — but more thoroughly!"

"Drugged?" cried Rosa Caporno. "Drugged?"

But she laid both hands to her forehead. I suppose that there was a weight of stupefaction in it.

"Yes," she said suddenly between her hands. "It is true!"

"Vidett!" said I.

"Señor?" she gasped at me.

"He tried with me, also. Luck saved me."

She stumbled past me and ran across her room to the open window. There she leaned out and drew in great eager breaths of the cool night air.

I had followed. She caught at me, found me,

231

and dragged me closer to her.

"What does it mean, señor?" said Rosa.

"I cannot tell. If I could tell, I should have stayed below to fight them."

"Them?"

"There are twenty men in the house of your father."

"Don Luis is leading them!"

"Vidett met them in the woods. I followed him there. I came back to the house. I found the room of your father locked and there was no answer when I called for him. I broke down the door and went in to him."

She had turned from the window and was staring at me, all unconscious of the water which dripped from her soaked clothes and body to the floor.

"I managed to bring him back to his senses for an instant. But then he was gone again. In that instant he said – 'the cellar.' "

"Yes!"

"As he closed his eyes again he whispered your name: 'Rosa.' I thought he was sending me to you to help him when he could not help himself. For even old Pedro has been drugged!"

"God forgive my sins!" whispered the girl. "Did Señor Caporno send you to me for help?"

"Yes."

She was extremely silent, breathing hard.

"He fumbled beneath his pillow – a key which he wanted was gone – stolen, he said."

"Don Luis would not dare –"

"Señorita, if there is anything to be done, act quickly. For I tell you that there is not much time. There is a very little time, only!"

"Hush!"

I listened.

"Do you hear?" said her whisper.

"Nothing."

"At the door of the room!"

I heard it then, the gliding step of a man, and then a faint sound of steel upon steel – the unmistakable sound of a key fitted into a lock.

"But the door is bolted, also!" said Rosa Caporno. "Ah, I have no weapons, but I have you, señor! Will you fight for me?"

"For your father, señorita, and for you, if you will let me!"

"For him – yes, and I shall fight for him, also – and is Luis –"

She choked on this and then raised a hand.

A soft voice was calling outside the door to her room – the voice of Lewis Vidett: "Conchita! Conchita!"

Very softly, and then the same call, more loudly.

The little maid ran to me instinctively for directions.

"Go," said I, "and open the door."

Rosa cast up a startled glance to me. But she did not countermand the order. The maid ran to the door.

CHAPTER 27

Rosa, with a sign, followed softly after – not a very romantically beautiful figure, I must admit, in her dripping clothes. But she was more than that to me. She was a girl in whom I was beginning to see an unsuspected honesty. She was in a position where I could enjoy her courage more, also.

"Conchita," came from outside the door. "Do you hear me?"

From the little *moza*: "Yes, señor."

"It is I – do you know me?"

"Señor Vidett."

"I must see your lady."

"She sleeps, señor."

"Wake her! Wake her! Instantly! I must speak with her to –"

"Señor, she is not well – she sleeps heavily!"

"Let me in, and I shall right that!"

"Admit you now? Señor!"

"In the name of heaven – little Conchita – little fool! How can I harm her?"

"I dare not."

"Let the door be unbolted, then, and let me pass you a restorative."

"But, señor, can you guess in what manner she is ill?"

"I can."

"This is wonderful, señor!"

"Little idiot! This will cost you your place if you keep tantalizing me in this fashion any longer!"

"You fill me with terror!" said Conchita, but the minx was fairly trembling with joy. It was apparent to me that she did not love the gentleman upon whom her mistress had been smiling so long. Feeling the shadow of my bulk coming up behind her, little Conchita cast up her head and smiled at me in the dim light which filled the chamber, and she found my hand and pressed it. She was a dear – that child. Full of courage and fear mixed. I thought her enchanting. Although she was much less lovely than her mistress, I thought her a great deal more intriguing.

"Will you open?" repeated Vidett. "I tell you, Conchita, it is a thing of the most vast importance. It is a thing which your lady –"

"I shall open, then," said the *moza* decidedly.

For I had made her a sign, and when the señorita questioned me, I repeated my gesture of command most emphatically. For I felt about the thing in this manner. No matter what the course of events might be before this fatal night was ended, it could not be other than an excellent thing for us to gain possession of the person of Señor Vidett. No matter what his relations might be with the score of armed men whom he had led so treacherously to the big house of Caporno, there was not a doubt that every one in the house would be better off if that leadership were removed from the twenty strangers.

Here Conchita shrank away from the door with a stifled cry, for out of the great distance, from an upper portion of the house, there was a sudden shout, followed by a thunderous, but dim trampling of feet. That sound spread, as a column of smoke spreads when it strikes against the ceiling of a room. Gradually sound and confusion covered the building.

I could hear Vidett cursing heavily outside the door of the room. "The dolts – the clumsy fools! The murdering, thick-hoofed swine!" groaned Vidett. "Conchita, open the door, or I shall break it down."

"Ah, no, señor! That would be a scandal, but as soon as I can turn the bolt –"

It was done at that moment. I had brushed Rosa back against the wall. She said to me one thing only: "No weapon, señor!"

"My hands, only!" I had answered.

I felt her soft hands flutter as lightly as the wings of moths against mine. Then, as she touched their weight, I heard her sigh.

"Be gentle with him – señor."

I reassured her with a murmur. But, in reality, my strange hatred of this handsome young man was turning my fingers into steel talons and my fist into the loaded head of a club. As the door opened, Vidett stepped in. Yet, in spite of all his haste, he did not step the full distance into the room. Had he done so, he would that instant have been lost, but, as it was, the hand with which I reached for him, fell a little short.

For I had supposed, from his eagerness, that he would rush headlong into the room. Who could keep from thinking the same thing? Yet he came in as stealthily as a robber.

So the first pass of my reaching hand missed his neck and brushed heavily across his face, knocking him aside against the door. The next instant a pistol spoke and a slithering tongue of fire and pain like the pain of hell went through my left leg.

I reached for him again with the scream of

Rosa tingling at my ear, but as the weight fell upon my left leg, it crumpled under the strain and I pitched to the floor upon my face.

"Ah, you have killed him!" I heard Rosa cry.

I heard the door slam – that was the hand of young Lewis Vidett, I knew. Then his voice.

"Who is it, in the name of the devil? No one but Mendez-Ames – whatever the fool's name may be! What are you doing here in the dark with him – what are the pair of you doing? No matter – he's done! When they fall on their face like this – the swine will suddenly –"

The toe of his boot found my ribs smartly.

It was a foolish move on the part of Señor Vidett. He should at the least have paid my size such a compliment as to put another slug or two into the bulk of me before he was sure that I was out of this world and in the next.

As he kicked me I felt no fury – I was only filled with an immense satisfaction. The back sweep of my long, thick arm – like a weaver's beam to one of the agile slightness of Vidett's body – knocked both his feet from under him, and he dropped not to the floor, but into my arms.

Rather the arms of an octopus for Vidett, than my arms at that moment. For the octopus reaches blindly, and I was using all the senses of triumph. Even so, with all the vast excess of my strength over him, it was not easy to master him. He whirled and twisted like a veritable eel. My first grip made the revolver fall out of his hand; but even in that swift, close melee he was able to get out a knife.

Before he could use it, however, I had him completely mastered, pressed close to my breast – and no lover ever held his mistress with a sweeter thrill of satisfaction than I now held the writhing body of Señor Vidett! I had one of his wrists tucked up in the small of his back, and a gesture of the hand which controlled that arm could fairly tear it out of its shoulder socket.

Vidett knew what had happened. He said without malice and without heat: "So – very well. You have me, señor."

"It is Mendez," said I.

"You are a spirit, not a man," said Vidett, still with that uncanny coolness. "How did you manage to clear your head?"

"I cleared it with the emetic, dear Vidett. It was clear when you came to visit me in my room."

"Ah, instinct, instinct!" cried Vidett softly to himself. "One touch of the knife then and you would have slept deeply and safely forever!"

I put all of this down as he said it, because

I wish to have you understand the satanic calm with which this man was able to conduct himself. Even as I held him at my mercy, I assure you that his words and the manner of them made my flesh creep.

I dragged myself to a kneeling position.

"Do him no harm!" Rosa was breathing in my ear.

"I shall not – unless he forces me to. But if you make a foolish move – I shall break you open like an oyster, Señor Vidett."

The devil actually laughed.

"You will find me more quiet than a very oyster!" he assured me.

"And you, Señor Mendez?" said the girl to me.

But I did not need to answer her. That little trump – that pearl among maids – that Conchita, had already found the trouble. Without a question asked, she had gone deftly over me and she had been able to locate the wound quickly enough by the great outpouring of blood.

"I have found it. Through the leg. I pray heaven that the bone be not broken!" she said. "Is the pain a frightful thing?"

It was very bad, and ordinarily, I suppose it might have almost overcome me. But one does not allow such a thing as pain to overcome one when there is a man like Lewis Vidett at hand! There was really a greater sense of pleasure than of pain at that moment.

"Rip off the leg of my trousers," I told Conchita. "Here is my knife. Señorita Rosa, bring a light. Will you permit me to fasten the hands of Señor Vidett?"

She hesitated one instant.

"Yes!" she said.

"Rosa!" cried my captive. "Without an explanation?"

She merely turned her back on him, and, running across the room, she picked up the lamp whose flame I had raised a moment before. With this in her hand she ran back to us and stood over the little group to give light to Conchita.

Conchita had my knife by this time. She made short work of that trouser leg. She peeled it off in no time, and I glanced down and saw the black blood bulging out of either side of my thigh.

Yet neither Conchita or Rosa were much disturbed. Rosa shuddered a little, but she held the lamp closer while Conchita ripped off an undershirt and with that formed the bandages.

I knew that a tourniquet was what would be needed, however. There was too much to be done in that house on that night, and I could not afford to be handicapped by a scratch in the leg. To me, in my excitement, that wound seemed no more!

I turned to help them at their work, for I had long before this secured the wrists of the excellent Vidett behind his back by means of a piece of twine which I always carry with me in my pockets.

CHAPTER 28

I turned my captive over to Conchita, first asking her if she felt able to control him. I offered her a revolver. She tried that cumbersome weapon with her small hand and then thrust it back at me.

"It'll do for those that like it," said she, "but I hate noise."

With that, she picked from somewhere in her clothes a knife as delicate and as keen as the last fine-spun icicle which hangs from the eaves, tapered to a paper thinness by a spring sun.

"This will do for me!" said that odd girl, and took her place at the back of her mistress' lover.

"You'll watch him well?" said I.

"Ay!"

"And remember that he's slippery?"

"I'll remember that he's a snake!" said she. "But my brothers used to catch snakes, and take their heads off. I've seen 'em do it!"

Whatever it was that Lewis Vidett had done to this girl, I could not doubt the reality of her hatred for him. Her upper lip quivered as she looked down at him, where he lay crushed on the floor.

In the meantime, Rosa had put down the lamp and she helped me in the arrangement of the tourniquet which was soon prepared. She furnished me with a little, stout paper cutter, and turning on this, with the bandage across the wound and above it, I put on such pressure that the flood soon stopped flowing.

There was plenty of cloth left. I made another bandage over the wound, in the hope of keeping some warmth in the wounded flesh, for I knew that there is a danger in catching cold in a wound. Then I used another part of the lengths of bandage for the purpose of making a stout sling. I tied my leg firmly at the ankle and again beneath the knee and fastened the ends of the strips of cloth to my belt. In this fashion, I was sure of keeping my leg above striking distance of the floor.

While I worked, I heard the muttered conversation between my prisoner and Conchita.

"Chita, one touch of that knife –"

"Why should I?"

"Because it will be worth a great deal to you."

"How should I be able to tell?"

"I give it to you beforehand!"

"I shall have a proof."

"But will you cut the cord that ties my wrists?"

He was so desperate that I suppose he dared to risk such loudness. Or was it that pain and fear had made any sense of hearing preternaturally alert on this night? At any rate, I heard him distinctly.

"Reach into the bag which is tied at my right hip!"

"Very well. What is there?"

"Take out a handful – softly – it is yours!"

Conchita, apparently, did as he directed her to do, and presently there was a shrill cry from her: Señorita! Señorita! You are robbed! Look what I have in my hand! He has robbed you of the three rubies and the only thing – "

Señorita Rosa, however much concerned she might have been over my wound – not sentimentally, but because I was simply her last resort as a defender on this night – flew to the side of her maid and I heard a low-pitched exclamation of surprise and of anger.

"Lewis!" cried she.

"And now, Rosa?" said that iron-nerved villain.

"Take the bag from his side," said Rosa Caporno.

"You need not look," said Vidett. "It is as you suspect. Everything is there."

"Ah, ah! The whole casket!"

"All of it, of course."

"And the reason, Lewis?"

Even I, no expert in affairs of women, could tell that there was danger in her voice at this point.

"The reason, my most dear child, is that in spite of our argument this evening, I decided that the thing must be done!"

"That we should leave the house?"

"Yes!"

"Unmarried, Lewis?"

"Unmarried, of course. Because we could be married within ten miles."

"Married within ten years – ten centuries!"

"Rosa, is there no love in you?"

"I almost wish that there were not, after to-night."

"No trust, then?"

"No, no, Lewis. I may have shown myself to you as a great fool, but never as such a fool that I would ever dream you were a man to be trusted!"

A sweet conversation to be carried on between ardent young lovers!

"Rosa, you deeply wrong me, my dear! Or is it because you have taken a liking to my dear friend Mendez – or Ames – whatever his true name may be – Mendez I am sure he is not!"

"Do not taunt me, Lewis," said she. "Whatever he is, he is merciful, and he did not tear out your throat when you lay helpless on the floor in his arms."

"Helpless? I?"

There was a groan from Vidett and then the snarling admission: "Ah, what a jackass I was not to strike him when the opportunity was presented to me! One more bullet as he sprawled on the floor. But by his manner of falling, I thought that the lout was dead! I had aimed for his heart!"

"Gentle Lewis!"

"Come, Rosa. We know one another!"

"Better every moment. Tell me now what your plan was?"

"I tell you simply: I would put you into a light sleep – "

"Light?"

"You are waked from it now, are you not?"

"Yes, that is true."

"Heaven's name – listen to the confusion in the house! The servants have been raised! There will be guns in a moment – Rosa, there is no time for explanations. Only trust yourself to my love!"

"Lewis, I love you until my heart bleeds. But I trust a cold stone more than I trust you!"

"I intended to gut the cellar of the house. The jewels were all that you and I could take with us."

"All? There is more than a million pesos worth of them! Far more!"

"Is it true, then?"

"Yes."

"The more reason, in the name of heaven, for you and for me to run together – with our sweet Conchita, also – to leave this stupid valley and the desert which you hate so much – and escape."

"With my father left behind? Lewis, you are clever, but he is wise. You might run fast, but he would find wings for his fat old body and overtake us! Do you not know him?"

"I know that he's dangerous, but I am no child. Every minute the danger grows – a warning may get to the town of San Marin. There may be armed men here at any moment – Rosa, Rosa, set my hands free and liberate me, or we are lost!"

She hesitated. I saw her slump to the floor beside him. She cast one guilty glance across her shoulder and toward me. I saw, then, that she had taken the knife from the hand of Conchita and the deadly edge of the steel was at the cord. One touch, and that serpent of a man would be free. One puff of her breath, after that, and the lamp would be out and the room lost in darkness. In such a fight in pitchy black, there was no doubt as to who would be the winner.

Yet I did not try to intervene. I supported myself on one leg with one hand and a shoulder spread against the wall. I kept the other hand on the butt of a revolver, but I did not draw it. I merely frowned down at her, and wondered.

"Señor Mendez!" came her cry to me. "What makes you trust me?"

"Because," said I, "I know that you are the daughter of Caporno, and I know that you love him as he loves you. You will not turn loose a rat to murder him!"

"No!" cried the girl. "I shall not. Lewis, it is true. You have robbed him, and you are too wise to leave this house without trying to make him harmless behind us. Tell me: You planned his murder in the end to make all safe?"

"It is false!" said Vidett.

"Will you swear?"

"I'll swear."

"But what is sacred to you?" asked the girl.

"The Bible, then."

But Rosa laughed. "The Bible? For you to make an oath?"

Suddenly an imp took me by the throat and made me cry out: "I've an oath for him. Will you swear by the blood of Truck Janvers – Crinky?"

I had fumbled blindly, maliciously, in the dark, never expecting that I could get any real response from a man so thoroughly on his guard against all things at all times. But I had a little overestimated the nerve strength of Crinky. It brought a sudden cry of agony from him and then a gasping voice:

"Truck Janvers – who in the devil's name –"

"Will you swear by that, Lewis?" asked the girl, although she shuddered, watching his emotion.

"No!" screamed Vidett suddenly. "But if I meant to finish him, it was because he needed finishing. Because I knew – from his own mouth – that he would never let us marry, Rosa! Because I knew that the old devil had planned to torment us a while longer and then slide me behind the bars of a penitentiary to get me out of your way! There's the truth, heaven help me!"

"That's the truth!" said Rosa with a savage quiver in her throat. "Ah, what a beast I've loved! What a beast I still love!"

She leaped up and stood back from him in horror. But as she stood beside me, there was such blind passion in her still, that she was sobbing softly and steadily with a heartbreaking grief.

Something else came before me through the darkness — the miracle of that fat man, Caporno, who in spite of his wickedness had been able to teach his cold-hearted daughter to love him with such a love!

CHAPTER 29

The bag of treasure which young Vidett had appropriated was now in the hands of his former lady love. She spilled out the contents on the couch, and I saw a dazzling river of color – green and red and yellow and blue and purest flashing crystal all jumbled together, quivering with brilliancy as the light in the lamp quivered a little and changed.

I did not have to be any judge of jewels to understand that this was a great wealth that I looked upon. A great wealth – perhaps the million that Vidett had mentioned.

Rosa scooped the jewels into the bag again and then stood over Vidett.

"You got the celler key from my father?"

"Yes," said Vidett sullenly.

"Where is it now?"

"The others have it."

"He lies," said I. "He would not trust it to

any other person, of course. He has it and we'll search him for it!"

"Keep off!" gasped Vidett. "I'd rather be filled with bullets than touched by a swine!"

The hatred of Vidett was like the hate of a snake. I felt half poisoned by it. But at least, I had the satisfaction of seeing the key in the hand of Rosa.

She kept it, but she gave the bag of treasure into my keeping.

"Good!" commented Vidett from the floor. "You trust him so much more than you can trust me, my dear Rosa?"

"I trust him because I have to trust him!" said the daughter of Caporno.

"Ah, Rosa, don't be a fool! Do you think that Mendez is here for anything more than the plunder he can get from you?"

"I do think that he is not!" she declared. "Señor, you are going down with me. If Conchita is not afraid to stay here with Vidett; and if you can drag yourself down the stairs."

"I am not afraid, señorita!" said the brave girl. "I am not in the least afraid. Believe in me! I shall keep him where he is. If he stirs, I shall have this knife ready – with your permission."

"You have my permission," said Rosa Caporno – and ah, but her voice was like chilled steel! "If he tries to trick you or to get away – strike home, Chita!"

A sibilant sigh from Vidett announced that in that instant he saw himself robbed of plunder, wife, and all future happiness. But Rosa left him without another word and we hurried out of the room.

I say that we hurried, though that is a strange name for it. A child could have moved faster. In the hallway, I had to throw my left arm over the shoulder of Rosa Caporno. She gave me an amazing strength to support and steady me as I hopped along on my one useful leg. But still she was not able to balance and control two hundred and twenty pounds of reeling bone and muscle, and our trail was the trail of a wriggling snake as we staggered down the corridors.

Before we reached the stairway, she announced her plan and her hope to me.

The key to the cellar was not the key to the ordinary cellar which extended beneath the house, but, far beneath that series of store chambers, there was another deep room, cut out of the solid rock and ventilated only by two small air passages, which were repeatedly fortified, throughout their length, by crossbars of steel. There was only one door leading to that subbasement, and the key was the one which opened the door – an affair a foot thick, and made of the finest iron and toolproofed steel. In that room, Rosa told me, were the treasure chests of her father, piled one on top of the other, chests each almost as secure as a separate vault, but all permeable, no doubt, by the instruments which had been brought by the assistants of Vidett.

From one of those boxes, which Vidett well knew beforehand, he had taken the jewel casket and gutted it of its contents, with a part of which he had tried to bribe that sturdily faithful little Conchita.

But there were very many of those boxes in the cellar. There were many and many of the chests, like trunks, but made of finest steel, and in these the possessions of her father were secured. What she hoped was that, since the plunderers had not been in the house very long, they would still be employed in tearing open the trunks one by one. A few of them might be scattered over the house, confining the servants to their rooms, or at least keeping them away from any intervention in the robbery. But the main group she hoped to find down in the subbasement still at their work, with the bulk of the treasure still unremoved.

"But," said I, "how can there be much more treasure than there is in this bag already?"

"Gold," said the girl. "A ton of gold, señor!

And paper money. They will hunt for that until they have found all of it. Vidett knew how much there was and he would have told."

We reached the stairway and here I gripped the balustrade's rail and with both hands on it swung myself down faster than the girl could run at my side. Yet it was hard work, and I had stopped at the first landing above the main hall to take my breath, with Rosa Caporno not half a step behind me, when I heard the steps of a man running up the stairs toward me. His head and shoulders came in view at that instant. He did not pause for a challenge. There was no purpose of questioning in his mind. He simply jerked up a revolver and smashed a bullet at my head.

It cut past my ear, a hair's breadth away.

I did not wait to parley, either. But I got him with a snapshot from the hip and cursed with satisfaction as I saw him fall.

But what a crashing he made! He tumbled backward, head over heels, his body crashing at full length on the broad steps until he floundered to a loose-jointed halt on the floor of the hall below.

"He is dead!" said Rosa Caporno savagely. "Thank heaven!" I echoed. And I struggled down the remaining flight of stairs to the hallway.

That shot had not startled any of the followers of Vidett, it seemed. They were either too far away in the house to hear the noise, or else the racket which had been raised in a dozen parts of the big building by this time drowned all the sound of the shots and the thundering fall.

We stepped over the body of that dead man and Rosa again put her whole strength under my left arm and we hobbled crazily away. She turned me down a cross corridor and so I came to the door of the room of Sam Clyde. I told the girl that I intended to go in to see how he was. She urged me bitterly to hurry on with her. Already we might be too late. As for this man, if Vidett had any real desire to finish him, there was no question as to what had happened to him long before this.

Still I insisted. I thrust the door open and a .45 Colt spoke from the dark.

"Clyde!" said I. "Are you going to murder your friends?"

"Mendez? Old-timer, I didn't know! I was taking no chances. A rat might of slipped into the room in the dark and gnawed the heart out of me before I knowed it!"

I hurried to him and leaned over the bed.

"How did you get the gun?" I asked him.

"I give five pesos to a sneakin', yaller-faced

skunk that come in here bringing my supper with him. He brung me the gat. And it ain't a bad one. Got a nice balance and –"

"Clyde, there's a gang of roughs looting the house. Vidett brought 'em."

"That's like him!"

"Tell me in one breath, if you can, what you know about him."

"I know enough to fix up a pretty fat book about that gent, and you can lay to that."

"You call him Crinky?"

"That was the nickname that his dad give him."

"Who was his father?"

"Truck Janvers. Ever hear of him?"

I forgot the stabbing pain of my wounded leg. I forgot the girl, waiting in the darkness behind me.

"Truck Janvers!" I breathed.

"Did you know him?"

"I was in the cabin the night he died. I saw the knife stick in his throat."

He said after a gasping moment: "I was down in the cabin the next day. It was me that buried poor old Truck. I seen that he wasn't knifed for his money. I figgered that it was something dirtier than that. So I come down on his trail. And when I got wind of Crinky –"

"His own father!" I groaned. For it was too

horrible to be true.

"Man, man!" muttered Sam Clyde. "You know nothin' about Crinky if you think that it bein' his father would stop him up any. Oh, no. He was right in there to play his own hand, and it didn't make no difference what stood between him and the thing he wanted. It was his old man threatening to tell in San Marin what he knew about Crinky that made Crinky decide to get rid of him! He wanted that talk stopped.

"It sure would of busted up the marriage if old Truck had wrote down to Caporno and told him about what sort of a sneak this here Crinky was. You see, Truck got married near thirty years ago, when he was all flush and hot after makin' a big gold strike. He got married to a pretty little French girl named Vidett. Well, she and Truck didn't get along none too well. A couple of years later she got a divorce and she took along with her the boy that was born.

"That's this Crinky. Truck didn't hear nothin' from him until he was pretty near a man, and after that the letters come pretty frequent − mostly askin' for money. Though there was a spell of quiet − three years when Crinky was in the pen −"

"Is it true?" asked the husky voice of the girl behind me.

"I'll give you my word and my oath, ma'am, whomsoever you might be –"

"Lie quiet!" I said to Clyde. "Señorita, let us hurry on. Still it may not be too late!"

CHAPTER 30

I had with me a very grim-faced girl as we reached the outer hall and turned down it again. She said not a word, but, now and again, a panting breath broke from her, and I knew that her spirit was on fire within her.

She led me, now, down a second flight of steps which penetrated to the first level of the basement; and then down a second flight which brought us to still another range of subterranean rooms. There was apparently a strong desire on the part of her father to establish suitable foundation before he built the house itself. I felt, as we turned down one twisting passage after another, as though we were in the midst of a labyrinth.

But the girl never paused. She hurried me on steadily until she came to a heavy door which she opened, and from beneath, through another door and down another short flight of steps, I heard a roar of voices. Not like twenty – but like two hundred!

A pair came laughing and singing up the steps toward the second massive door, which stood ajar. They were carrying some heavy burden between them – I could tell by their grunting and by the slowness with which they mounted.

What it was they bore upward could be readily guessed by stout canvas hampers, which stood on the steps of the stairway beside us. Rosa Caporno flipped open one of the covers and threw the flash of an electric torch into the interior. And I saw the dull, rich glimmer of bar gold within – a shallow layer, but a ponderous one, no doubt!

So I swung myself down clumsily – for there were no railings on either side of the stairs, and I reached and drew open the great second door. A foot thick, indeed, but by its weight I rather judged it to be made of lead than of steel.

It came slowly back and just before me I saw two well-masked men, swaying and staggering with the weight of their burden as they reached the upper landing.

I had a revolver in my hand, but I could not shoot. I think that I was not born with a reluctance to take life, but too long familiarity with danger and death had taken from me all impulse to destroy. There was no need here. I could hurt them terribly enough with the gun as a club. I steadied myself against the wall with one hand and with the other dashed the gun into the face of the nearest bearer. I felt bone give to the stroke – mouth and nose must have been beaten in by the blow, and he fell with a muffled scream of pain behind his mask.

The second man had torn out his own weapon when I reached for him, but before he could press the trigger I had fetched him a slap beside the head with the long, heavy barrel of the Colt. It flipped him from the unrailed stairway and I heard his body strike with a sickening heaviness and dullness on the floor beneath a moment later.

By this time there had been warning enough to the others below. Three men came crowding into view, guns in hand, as I strained the door forward. I had no need of my own Colt. I let it fall and gave both my hands to the work which lay under them. That was ample! I could have sworn that there were resisting hands on the other side of the door, dragging back against me.

The guns barked in a rattling volley beneath me. Two bullets ripped through the screen of thin board on the inside of the door and hugged flatly against the heavy face of metal beneath.

The third slug was better aimed. It sliced a furrow across my cheek.

But that was nothing. They would do no more than scratch the surface of my flesh if they got to me before the door was closed. Now there were half a dozen flying up the stairway toward me.

The door was now swaying so far shut that it was a screen against their bullets, however. Here was Rosa at my side, moaning with eagerness and throwing all her weight into the work, while the giant door screamed wildly on its rusted hinges and slowly, slowly drew toward a close.

It was almost shut. Rosa gave up her work of pushing and, fixing the key in the lock, stood ready to turn the wards as soon as the door was shut. Then – with only an inch more to go – two men struck the door together, giving it the solid shock of their shoulders. My forward progress was stopped. Two or three more slammed against it from the other side and I was jarred back a whole foot!

There I held them! With all my force centered in one single leg, I thrust back at them, and a giant came into me and made the door lock in its place. Here a hand appeared around the edge of the door and a gun in it. The gun fell undischarged and the hand was withdrawn with a scream of pain, for Rosa Caporno had buried the length of a keen knife in the wrist!

The exclamation of the wounded man – and perhaps he stumbled against one of those who were thrusting at the door – made them relax their efforts. Or perhaps it was the confusion, for every man down in the subcellar seemed to know what the meaning behind that closing door was – sure death or capture for them!

And they came in a massed swarm up the steps, yelling with desperate fear. In that instant of weakness – of confusion – of alarm – whatever it was, I leaned all my weight against that door with a lunging force that made the tendons crack in my leg. Yes, if I had had a sound body to throw into my work, I think that I could have made head against twenty of them, I was so desperate. But even as it was, I seemed to take balance – and the door shuddered its way shut. Only an instant, but in that instant the ready hand of the girl had turned the great key and the lock had immediately shut home with a loud clang.

Like the distant murmur of bees, blown on a wind from the lowland, so we heard the wild scream of despair which rose from the men in the treasure chamber. Yet they were a scant foot away from us. But what a foot of solidest steel! Sound could not penetrate it! Rather it was a small vibration than a sound.

Then I turned to the girl and she – well, I suppose it was the hot Spanish blood in her which made her impulsive – but she threw her arms around my neck and kissed me.

It isn't very gentlemanly to confess, but I have to say that I merely pushed her away from me. I had started the double wound in my leg bleeding by the strain of closing that door. More than that, I had started a ready flow of the keenest agony. I was a sick man as I thrust Rosa Caporno away from me.

"Get me up!" said I faintly. "I feel that I'm dying, Rosa Caporno!"

"You'll not die. A hundred like Lewis Vidett and his kind could never be the death of such a man as you! You can't die."

She locked my left arm over her back and so we struggled toward the head of the stairs – but I was dreadfully weak now, with the labor, the nerve strain of that horrible night, and the drain of lost blood.

Then, as we gained the top of the stairs – surely there was a providence in that! – a light, bounding form of a man came hurrying toward us.

"Lewis Vidett!" gasped the girl at my side, and by the strangled sound of her voice I knew

267

that she had seen and heard enough to kill all her old love for the man at last. There was only horror of him remaining.

I felt my own strength flood back on me: "Vidett!" I thundered at him.

He stopped and leaped to the side like a dodging rabbit.

I held my gun poised. I cannot tell why I did not shoot at once. I knew the man was a deadly fighter. But somehow, as the girl shrank from my side, a frightful sense of certainty came upon me, and I knew that I had the life of Lewis Vidett in my hand. I knew that I could kill him if I chose to kill. I chose.

He had fired as he dodged, fired with a cry of savage hatred. That bullet plucked at the clothes at my side – a narrow miss. I pulled my own trigger, then – the hammer stuck, and then descended slowly – the gun had gone wrong!

His weapon spoke again, and this time a ripping pain sawed through my body – I did not know where. Sawed through me, as a lightning flash saws through the heart of the heavens.

There was nothing left for me to do. I hurled the gun in his face and he went down heavily on the floor. Then I lurched toward him, falling as I lurched, for I was quite off balance, on my one leg.

And he? He was wriggling up the instant his knees struck the floor of the hall.

My frantic reach toward him secured no more than a tip of the finger's hold on the edge of his coat. But that was enough!

First he strove to spring back, but in that instant I freshened my grip to a whole handful of cloth. He fired a second bullet into my body.

Too late, my beautiful Vidett!

The sway of my shoulder jerked him down into my arms. No matter if my body was gone – sick and numbed with pain! For my arms were still sound and strong. Under the pressure of their grip, like the weight of tons upon him, Vidett crumpled. I heard him gasp against my breast. His gun slid out of his lifeless hand. I could have picked it up and put a bullet through him, but I did not. For I thought that as I lay there, throwing all my might into that mortal grip – I thought as I lay there that I felt his heart beat heavily once against mine, and then stop.

And I was right.

They put us in one room. On one bed lay Sam Clyde. On the other bed lay Hugo Ames, alias Francisco Mendez. But as I came out of the time of fever, I found that Sam Clyde had quite recovered and sat up by my bed – recovered so far, at least, that he could sit up with his wounded leg resting on another chair and his crutches resting behind his shoulder. There he was sitting when the good, clean senses returned to me at the end.

"Well, Ames," said he, "how are you now? Better, lad?"

I stared feebly up at him, trying to rally my wits, and the first thing I realized was that he should be calling me Mendez rather than Ames.

I raised a hand to my face and it touched the naked skin. Then I saw it all. They had shaved my face on account of the wound in my cheek, and that shaving had exposed to their eyes a face which was too well-known by poster in a hundred crossroads. Ames, with fifteen thousand dollars on his poor life!

"They know?" said I.

"Everything," he said, grinning, "and the whole household knows!"

"I'm done, then?" said I.

"Son," said he, "these here Spanish speaking folks ain't like us. Some ways they're worse. Some ways they're better, and if one of the servants in this here house was to blow the truth about you, he'd have his throat cut by one of his pals, and he knows it. Specially a rider

named José. He has been tellin' r
you took care of him and how
by swiping Spike."

That was enough. I saw old
ward and he told me that I had sa
tune, his life, and his daughter's happ⌐
said it as shortly as that.

"Now," said he, "will you settle down w⌐
us, my son? I want you, because of all the
chance investments I ever made you were the
most chancy and you worked out the best!
Because, my boy, from the first day I knew that
you were Ames!"

That was enough to stagger me. If I had not
been sick, I suppose that it would have made
me sick to hear him say that. I told him, however, that although I appreciated his kindness,
his ways were not my ways and that the best
thing for me was to get well and travel back
north to my own mountains.

I was surprised when he agreed with me very
heartily.

"Horses with horses and dogs with dogs!"
chuckled Caporno. "You're right! The first day
you can ride, you start."

I started. But, in addition to Spike between
my knees, I carried away with me a bank
receipt for five thousand dollars.

Altogether, I was a lucky fellow. But I was

271

be done with it all, and I never left any
so gladly as I left the great house and the
smile of Caporno. May I never see him
ain!